# to the bridge

## Luke Andreski

DarkGreenBooks

*to the bridge*

Published by **Dark Green Books**

**Dark Green Books** are an imprint of the Authors and Writers Distribution Service

Second Edition, November 2017
ISBN 9781973473121

This publication or download is a work of fiction. All the characters, events, bodies, objects, avatars, organisations, establishments, personal stigmata or other details contained in this work, other than those clearly in the public domain, are fictitious. Any resemblance to actual persons, living or dead, is purely coincidental.


978 1 9734731


Copyright © Luke Andreski 2017

Luke Andreski has asserted his right under the Copyright, Designs and Patents Act 1988 to be identified as the author of this work.

All rights to publication, distribution or serialisation, in any form or in any media, are reserved by the copyright holder. No part of **to the bridge** may be reproduced, stored in a retrieval system, or transmitted in any form, or by any means, electronic, mechanical, recording or otherwise, without the prior permission in writing of Luke Andreski. Electronic copies may be purchased from www.lukeandreski.com but are sold for sole use only and must not be copied for the use of anyone other than the purchaser or as a once-only gift from the purchaser to one other person for their sole use.

www.darkgreenbooks.co.uk
info@darkgreenbooks.co.uk

# Part One
# Journeys One, Two and Three

*to the bridge*

## Chapter One

Everything has meaning. There is meaning in the speck in your eye, in the way you blink at an uncomfortable moment. The fragment of a half-remembered dream contains meanings you will never dare investigate. Before a thing has happened it has meaning. Somewhere a home awaits it. When the dust has settled, its name tag is revealed.

For Michael there was meaning in the way the door was double-locked.

The staleness of the air in the hallway held ineluctable meaning. It made of Michael Germain a child, lonely and ashamed; transformed his home into a boarding school, all visiting parents gone.

The note was waiting for him on the kitchen dresser. A cold white light – overflowing with meaning – shone between the slats of the wooden blinds. Michael walked to the dresser, picked up the note, held it before him like a book of prayer.

The note said almost nothing.

Less than nothing.

For Michael there was more meaning there than words could ever have conveyed.

Sarah had used a black biro. Had written carelessly, as if in a hurry. It was her reckless, postcard script: the cross of the t flying over the length of the word; no dot above the i.

She'd signed herself 'Sarah'. Not 'Your darling'. Not 'Love, Sarah'. Not 'Sarah xxx'.

Just 'Sarah'.

He screwed up the sheet of paper, threw it in the bin.

No subtle meaning there…

It was normal now, to treat Sarah's notes as if they meant nothing, to stroll to the bin, to discard them.

Its normality held a world of meaning. It was a statement – ringing like the bell of a buoy in deep fog – of loss.

*to the bridge*

Later, Aunt Mildred would read about that moment in the diary Michael kept. She would read:

> Sarah might as well have written "Goodbye forever"… She might as well have written "You are a stranger to me now. For the rest of our lives it will be as if we had never touched, as if we had never been utterly close. For the rest of our lives it will be as if we had never made love".

Mildred would read in the next paragraph:

> She might as well have written "Fuck you".

The kettle's automatic sensor no longer worked. The thing would boil half away before realising what was happening and turning itself off. Michael walked over to it now, brought its turbulence to an abrupt and sudden end.

He drowned a teabag in scalding water. Drifted, cup in hand, into the lounge. Lowered his cup onto the coffee table. Picked up the phone.

He closed his eyes. Held the phone before him like a tablet of stone – like a testament gifted, without intermediaries, from the hand of God.

There were questions he wanted answered.

Quite a number of questions.

Important questions.

He opened his eyes, admired the seamless ergonomics of the phone.

He wanted to know why anything was worthwhile.

He wanted to know – in a world where some people had everything and others had nothing – why the people who had everything still managed to be unhappy.

He wanted to know why – for almost all his life – he had never been able to appreciate anything until it was gone.

He wanted to know why Sarah had never wanted children.

He wanted –

He keyed in a number.

He liked the older phones – to have to key in numbers rather than utter a name and let the phone dial itself.

Soon incomplete syllables would be all that was needed – or even just thought – and nanotechnology would fathom your innermost intention and establish lines of communication on the basis of an algorithm of what it is to be human.

Soon –

'Hello?'

His mother's voice.

There were other things that he wanted to know, other things that the cordless, inarticulate phone needed to explain to him.

He wanted to know why anything meant anything, if anything really meant anything at all…

He wanted to know why TV presenters were more entitled to their opinions than Mary Nice-But-Dim next door.

He wanted to know why one opinion, in a world drowning in opinion, should have any more weight than any other.

He wanted to know why he couldn't help but go on eating crap which made him overweight when he knew full well that millions of people in Africa looked like Sarah had when she was ill in hospital but not because of chemotherapy but because they had never ever had enough to eat.

He wanted to know why somewhere in the core of his soul he had never believed that he deserved to be loved.

He wanted –

'Mum?'

'Michael? Is that you?'

'Yes, it's me. Michael.'

He wanted to know why something close to fear echoed in his mother's voice whenever she realised who it was who was phoning her.

'Michael! What's wrong?'

Now, there was a question…

*What's wrong?*

She had always been that sort of mother. 'What on earth is wrong, Mikey?' she would have said a few years ago, when he was still a child. 'Why are you making such a fuss?'

'It's – it's Sarah, mum.'

'Is something wrong with Sarah? Something new?'

And there was another question worth asking.

*Is something wrong with Sarah?*

He wished he could tell his mother what had happened – the whole story, unabridged – but he couldn't find the words. All of a sudden he felt a desperate need to put down the phone, to listen to the silence that had crept over the house, to try to work out what it all meant... but it was too late to stop. His conversation was gathering its own momentum. It was all set to carry on by itself, independently of anything Michael could do, ricocheting away through the ether no matter what.

'No, mum,' Michael's voice said, translated by the phone into zeros and ones, 'there's nothing's wrong with Sarah. Nothing at all. She's left me, that's all. Sarah's left me.'

*Sarah's left me.* The words echoed somewhere in his head, echoed back to him from the phone. This wasn't communication. He had known it wouldn't be. When he spoke to his mother it never was.

This was action and reaction – a reflexive response to the shapes of words. He had known how his mother would react, what she would think. It was utterly predetermined. It was irrevocably shaped by everything that had happened in the past.

*The little bitch,* is what she would think. *My darling boy... The little bitch...*

She would think murderous thoughts. Maternal defensiveness, the possessiveness of the matriarch, would already have been triggered in her mind – would be jerking his mother about like a puppet at the end of instinctive, predetermined strings.

*The little bitch.*
*My darling boy.*
*The little bitch.*


'Sarah's left you?' his mother asked.

Michael thought he could hear the grinding of her teeth. 'Yes,' he said.

'The – oh, the little cow! Oh, Michael, I'm so sorry! How could she be so stupid? How could she do this to you? Oh, darling! It's so far from being what you deserve! After all you've done for her! After everything you did while she was ill! Oh, Michael... Oh, Michael, I never really thought you could trust her, you know that, not really. You know that's what I've always thought. This is just – this is just what I expected all along. Oh, Michael! Oh, you poor, poor boy!'

*You poor, poor boy.*

Michael bridled at the phone.

*Telecommunications...* he thought. *Whose clever idea was that?*

'I'm not a boy, mum – and it's not what *I* expected. It's the last thing I expected. In fact, it's not even entirely true.'

'Michael, are you crying?'

Mildred, 'Auntie M', would read in Michael's diary:

> I should never have phoned up mum.
> Did I think I could just say goodbye, could just shut her down?
> Mum's inescapable. She's in my blood. The years of my upbringing have imprinted her upon my brain.

He said, 'You've got it wrong, mum. She hasn't really left me. Not physically.'

'Michael, what's wrong? What do you mean "Not physically"?'

'She's left me in the only way that matters, mum. She – she's stopped loving me. Sarah doesn't love me any more...'

'Oh, Michael... Oh, my poor boy...'

'And there's more.'

'Oh darling...'

'You see, I don't really blame her. *I* would walk away from the person I've become if I only had the strength. You see, I've realised something important, mum. I've realised I'm not worthy of love – not of Sarah's love, not of anyone's love. I wonder if that's what you taught me, all those years ago? I wonder if that's the lesson my childhood imprinted on me? I'm a worthless little shit, mum, that's what I've realised. I'm small, mum, a small business man with the emphasis on *small*... I've – I've had enough, mum. I've had enough of struggling to be something that I know I'm not. I want out. That's what I want. That's all I want. I want out. Out of here. Out of telecommunications. Out of everything.'

'Oh, Michael! What did Sarah say? What did the little bitch say?'

'She's not a bitch. She didn't say anything. I'm fucked, mum, that's all. That about sums it up... I'm totally and utterly fucked.'

'Michael! Don't say that, my darling! You're not... bloody *effed*. You've never been... *effed*. Maybe – maybe, Michael! – maybe you're just seeing something wonderful and new! Maybe this is just the beginning of something different, my darling! Even if Sarah does leave you, this could be a fresh start, a new opportunity, a time for change. You're not *fucked*, Michael – of course you aren't! Maybe this is God intervening at last! Maybe there will be something new for you now – something more meaningful, something better than you have ever had before!'

'Like you, mum?'

'Michael – I'm just trying to help! You know that! All I'm trying to do is help!'

*Help...*

*What a funny word.*

*It didn't sound quite right.*

*It sounded like a cross between a greeting and a kind of seaweed.*

*"Hello."*

*"Kelp."*

*"Help..."*

*What does it mean?*

'Help?' Michael asked. '*Help*'s not what I need... And in any case there's nothing left to help. There's nothing left to salvage. The person you could have helped is gone. I love Sarah. I've always loved her. I loved her before she was ill. I loved her all the time she had cancer. I love her now. But she doesn't love me. Not any more. She doesn't love Michael Germain and there's nothing I can do about it. I've tried to salvage something – I've tried everything I could possibly have tried – but I've failed. She's closed me out, mum. She's shut me out completely, and I can't find a way back in. It's like I've never really been here, in this house, in our home. It's like I've ceased to exist. It's – '

He was no longer making sense.

He knew that now.

His tongue was clattering in the sterile spaces of his mouth. His teeth were moon rocks in a desolate lunar landscape. His body was a spacesuit from which the air was steadily escaping. That was the hiss he could hear down the telephone line. It wasn't static. There is no such thing as static anymore. That hiss – that was his voice.

'I love you, mum,' he said or maybe shouted. He needed to shout to hear his own words. Could his mother hear him? He doubted if she could – and he didn't think she would want to hear whatever it was he was saying anyway. He was tumbling over and over like an abandoned space station, halfway between the sun and the earth, a spurious historical artefact. The meanings of his words were tumbling in and out of the sound that they were making, reverberating through the narrow corridors they were allowed to occupy, the sounds sounding senseless, conveying nothing of the love or pity or self-pity or anger or whatever emotion it was that he was trying to convey.

What were they? What were his *words*? What in any case could they have possibly hoped to convey?

A cry of loss? An expression of desolation?

Hope?

'I love you, mum.'

He doubted if even that was true. It was just more air escaping, a hissing, sibilant noise, very far away. He no longer understood its meaning, though in itself it must have had meaning. There is meaning in everything.

Ineluctable meaning.

He put the phone down suddenly. Picked up his cup of tea.

A fair exchange, he thought.

A telephone for a cup of tea.

Stared at the tense unbroken surface of the drink.

There was only one person he had ever truly loved.

Sarah was the only person he had ever truly loved.

He loved his wife, Sarah. Only ever Sarah.

But Sarah no longer loved him.

'I'm fucked, mum,' he said to his mother, or seemed to remember saying.

'That's what I am. That's all I am…

'Fucked.'

## Chapter Two

Even when they were enemies, even when they loathed one another and did not speak, when they sat at opposite ends of the room and avoided one another's gaze, even then Mildred had always been there for Jane. She was an inescapable mirror that would suddenly surprise Jane when she paused to glance aside: selective in what it chose to reflect, offering insights that were usually unwanted, that were almost certainly unasked for.

Jane was surprised now – taken aback, really – at how old Mildred looked.

*Am I that old? Is that how I have begun to look?*

'What are you reading?' she asked, hiding her concern.

Mildred refused to look up. 'You know what I'm reading. I've been reading it for weeks. Quarantine by Jim Crace.'

'I've read that, surely? Years ago?'

'Michael gave you a copy. Don't you remember?'

'I can't remember reading it. Or… or perhaps I vaguely remember not greatly enjoying it.'

'I will probably like it, then…'

*You bitter old crone,* Jane thought, and, in reprisal, said, 'You're looking old, Millie, if you don't mind my saying so… Far older than your age. It worries me.'

Mildred lowered her book at last and met Jane's gaze. They were seated in Jane's sitting room. They were sisters-in-law, not sisters, but from their ability to sit silently together you might not have guessed it. They had been drinking Earl Grey tea. 'So it was Michael on the phone," Mildred said. "Hostility is always how you respond after talking to that son of yours.'

'Yes. Poor Michael…'

'And what has he done to upset you this time?'

'Nothing whatever. He hasn't upset me.' Jane shifted uncomfortably. She hated Mildred's penetrating, *I know you better than you know yourself* stare. 'He hasn't upset me at all. Not even slightly.'

And of course she wasn't upset. Why should she be? She wrapped her arms around her chest and sank back into the sofa. Not *upset*, she mused, but somehow... *estranged from herself...* Somehow *estranged* from the world. She felt old, cold, sterile. As sterile as an item of laboratory equipment, that was how she felt. As sterile as a Petri dish or a measuring beaker, as callipers, a scalpel. As cold as ice in the Antarctic. Colder. As cold as the interstellar spaces beyond the far side of the moon. Or colder even than that. The distant memory of her menopause seemed attractively redolent of turbulence and heat. She felt as old and cold and sterile as Mildred must feel, she thought. Maybe older.

Maybe colder.

Maybe more sterile.

Michael had always been such a good boy. Recently she had begun to hope that he might follow her to God, that he might return with her to the arms of the church. What a consolation that would be! Some of the things he had said, some of the questions he had asked, pointed, she told herself, towards a questing soul. Pointed, she had told herself, towards an uneasy heart harkening for its everlasting home.

Was Michael testing her, she wondered? Was that what the phone call had been about? Was he trying to fathom the inner peace which she had gained from believing in Christ?

What a jealous, stirring longing that thought kindled in her heart!

Was Michael ready at last to recognise a greater truth: that Sarah had only ever been a distraction? That the real focus of his dedication and love should be – could only ever be – the god of creativity, and God Himself?

*Never mind,* she thought. *Never mind what that attractive little bitch has accomplished over the years, the damage she has done. Michael will return to the welcoming arms of his mother, and I will be the ones who looks after him. I will be the one who shows him the way to absolution.*

What were children, after all, if not God's greatest gift? And just as God was Father to the Saviour, so Jane's mission would be to care for her son. God had taken His child back to Him. Following His example was the least that Jane could do...

She glanced at Mildred, picked up her rosary, began checking over the beads.

Mildred glowered over the top of her book. 'Satan's necklace,' she muttered. 'Put it away, Jane. You know how much it irritates me when you fiddle.'

'This isn't fiddling, this is prayer.'

'Then pray elsewhere.'

'Why on earth do you hate Jesus so much?' Jane asked. 'Why can't you leave Him alone?'

Mildred smiled. It was like the blade of a knife slipping gently between Jane's ribs. 'I only wish I knew, dear. Perhaps it's because I find it difficult not to see the ridiculousness of it all… it's absurdity… particularly when adopted by a long-term and once fervent atheist.'

'I've never been an atheist! And definitely not a fervent one.'

'Oh, I think you have. Let's not be too eager to re-write history.'

'A sceptic is how I would have described myself at the very worst – or perhaps an agnostic.'

'And now, once again, a Catholic.'

'Isn't a person allowed to return to the fold?'

'Then let me hear your confession, old girl. Explain to me how an intelligent person can believe such impossible rubbish.'

'I believe what I believe because I have seen in my heart that it's true. '

'Well, believe that if you wish. I have seen in my heart that it's nonsense of the first water. They call that a Mexican stand-off, dear. We each have a gun pointed at each other's beliefs. Your son's wife had cancer. Michael will never have children. You will never have grandchildren. Your husband left you years ago and your great genetic journey has come to an end. Have all those things been sanctioned by your almighty and benevolent God?'

'I think so… yes.' Jane's fingers passed over the beads. For her, in an unorthodox way, each bead seemed to be a statement of the integrity of the self. For her each bead offered Jane Germain, divorcee and mother, redemption, forgiveness and absolution from guilt. How many beads should she savour, she wondered? *In how many ways have I failed my son?*

In the currency of human warmth Jane had been short-changed. She had been born with hardly any warmth to give – barely enough to keep even her own poor soul warm. And what can you do when God short-changes you, other than believe in Him? Who else could possibly have been the author of such injustice? Who else but God can help you reinterpret your weakness as a different kind of good? And, hanging from her neck, a wooden cross, its arms outstretched to embrace mankind. 'Come unto me,' it whispered in its close proximity to her heart. 'Come. Let me measure the worth of your soul.'

'Satan's abandoned him,' she said.

'A nice slip,' Mildred said with a snort. 'Or have you really resorted to calling her that?'

'Sarah. Satan. They're much the same…'

Mildred lowered the novel Quarantine onto her lap. 'So she's left him… You'll be pleased, then.'

'I *was* pleased. I was pleased when I heard him say those words. I couldn't help myself… But now I feel guilty about my reaction. It's uncharitable of me. Godless. He was crying, you see, Millie. Michael was crying like a little boy.'

'He was always one for crying, as a boy.'

'He said… Michael said… that he was *fucked*. Then he put down the phone.'

Mildred smiled again. It was the old, cynical smile that Jane knew so well. *Old, though*, thought Jane. *'Old' is the operative word.*

For there were no longer any unlined spaces between the lines that made up Mildred's face. Wrinkles curved back from her eyes and around her cheeks. Others swept out in near parallel bands across her forehead, vanishing somewhere beneath her thinning hair. Everywhere, wrinkles, like a shrunken apple. Yet, at the heart of it all, her eyes were as ageless and intelligent and lovely as they had ever been.

*That's how I must look,* Jane thought. *That old. Or will it take me another two years, or four, or five, to catch up with her? Or am I already farther gone than she is? Am I simply indulging in wishful thinking in supposing I look younger?*

Mildred took off her reading glasses. She returned Jane's stare while Jane rolled the beads of the rosary between her fingers, searching endlessly for a flaw that might give her ascendancy at last, that might offer some brief interlude, some hope of escape from the sterile wasteland her life had become without a husband, with a stolen son.

'He doesn't mean *he's* fucked, dear,' Mildred said. 'That's not what he means at all.'

'Tell me, then, since you clearly understand my son better than I do…'

'Well, it's not *I'm fucked*. Oh, no, that wouldn't be Michael at all. Not at all.' Mildred's smile broadened. She was about to deliver the killing blow – and Jane could sense its meteoric approach from at least one million miles before impact.

'No, dear. It's quite clear what that son of yours means. Not *he's* fucked, no. What Michael *really* means, dear, is *fuck you*.'

'Fuck you? What rubbish!'

'No, that's precisely what he means. Fuck you, world. Fuck you, family and friends. Fuck all of you – I'm off.'

## Chapter Three

It had taken such a long time to get to this place.

They had met thirteen years ago – at the tail end of his interminable affair with Tabitha. Tabitha had been Yoko Ono to Michael's John Lennon, an odyssean siren who never let him make love to her but who always summoned him back when she thought he was beginning to stray. An Israeli with a German name, he used to whisper, 'My little leibling. Ich bin meine eine leibling.' And she had whispered back, 'Okay, smarty-pants. I'll be your German mistress if you'll be my French resistance fighter.'

'Mais oui, Madamoiselle.'

In those words lay the secret of their relationship. It was an unyielding war of resistance, dramatic in its foreplay but eternally inconclusive in its consummation. It was Palestine v. Israel, Chechnya v. Russia, Afghanistan versus Great Britain and the United States.

Tabitha was younger than Michael, slim and strong and built for speed. Her hair was as thick and black and short as a boy's. Convinced he was in love with her, he remained, all the same, in a permanent state of withdrawal. It was as if he knew, in some machine-gun emplacement at the perimeter of his mind, that their relationship could never last… and that he needed to hold in reserve the capability for a pre-emptive strike.

What a fool he had been in those rash, impetuous days! He had loved throwing his money around, what little he had. He had been loud, profligate, extrovert, an incurable flirt. Bring on the good-looking woman and whoa! just look at how attentive he became! how helpful! how gentlemanly! – though always with a predatory eye focussed on the upshot. He should have warned the girls he flirted with that you can never trust a man who always smiles. He should have worn a placard across his shoulders saying, 'Don't turn your back on me. I bite.'

With a super-sensory understanding of the subliminal messages of his success, whenever Rachael or Margie or Emma began to return Michael's attentions, his little Israeli girl would summon him back – and back he would come, a stranger suddenly to Suzie or Peta or Jane, their barely ignited infatuation abandoned, their briefly roused passion spent. And reeling him in like a half-drowned shark, Tabitha would remind him of how much in love they were, and allow him brief access to the haven of her bedroom, and murmur in his ear, and explore with her fingertips the ladder of his spine – and that would be that. Even then, even when he had prostrated himself before her and given up everything for her, they never made love. Never properly. Never fully. Never to Michael's satisfaction.

Not even in the end.

Tabitha had been twenty-three years old and intent upon saving herself for her wedding night. 'You must marry me first,' she had whispered to Michael. 'Convert to Judaism… and then we'll marry… and after that… well, we'll see…'

She'd said, 'The best things in life are always worth waiting for, don't you think?'

Michael would tell himself later that Tabitha must always have known that she couldn't keep him hanging on forever. Both of them, in their heart of hearts, must surely have realised that 'No' so often repeated meant 'You're not the one'. That 'Not yet' so adamantly insisted upon surely meant 'Never'. That 'I'm not ready' could only ever have implied 'There is something about you that I don't really like'.

Tabitha had always known that she was Little Miss Right. She had always been – and still was, in Michael's mind, even after all these years – the symbol of everything that was desirable and intelligent and sexy. How could she have failed to know that she hadn't found her equal? How could she have doubted that she hadn't met her match?

And how could Michael ever have hoped to be anything better than Little Miss Right's big Mister Wrong?

He met Sarah on a tube train. Met her… saw her… first became acutely aware of her on a tube train somewhere near Ealing Broadway. She hurried onto the train and sat down close by, almost opposite him. She had been running – perhaps running to catch the train – and was attractively out-of-breath. She wore a short skirt, a halter top that did little to reduce the impact of her breasts. Knee-high lace-up boots and the sheen of satin enforced Michael's undivided attention. He was struggling not to obsess with the shadowy line between her thighs when her mobile rang. It gave him a nasty jolt. She had probably seen him staring at her like an idiotic schoolboy, drawn in by the promise of fabric and flesh. What would she think? How deeply would she despise him? He looked away – and listened intently as she chattered to some friend or acquaintance, her voice cheerful and light-hearted. When the conversation ended, she lowered the phone from her ear, looked at him, looked away, and then, amazingly, sat there with tears running down her face. She made no attempt to wipe them away. It happened three times. At the next station she was on the phone again, calling someone back: seeming animated, seeming happy despite the tears drying on her cheeks, seeming not to have a care in the world. Michael couldn't help but feel, as she chattered away, that her world was one full of laughter and smiles. Then, abruptly, she was weeping again, the conversation ended, the phone clutched tightly upon her lap. It was like watching some strange natural phenomenon – like watching a spider spin its web on the wing-mirror of a speeding car. Mended... broken... mended... broken... each condition adjacent in time but dimensionally utterly separate. Mesmerised, he even followed her out of the tube station and down to Ealing Broadway, then on, past the council building and the library to where the shops began to peter out.

He hadn't been certain how he felt. Fascination at her unashamed manipulation of her moods? Sympathy at her struggle to cope with the pain some turncoat relationship had set her up for? His opening gambit, when she realised he was following her, was, 'I just wanted to ask if you're okay?' And then, when she shook her head, 'Can I walk you home?'

What he'd really wanted to say was, 'Just tell the bastards to piss off. I'll look after you... if you'll let me.'

In his diary he would write:

> When Sarah looked at me that first time it was as if a door had opened between two phases of my life. Light came streaming through, out of the future, into the past. It showed Tabitha as hopeless, unattainable, flawed. It showed my former self, the person I had been up until then, as a child. There, beyond the door, was someone new, someone stronger than before, someone wearing my face but with my father's strength, my father's charisma. It was the person I should have always been – had always wanted to be. The person Sarah and only Sarah

could allow me to become. Tabitha no longer had the power to hold me after that. The cord was cut. I was free at last.

Barely a week later, Tabitha was the one who was crying in front of him – clutching at his hand as he tried to pull it free, her face crumpled up like a child's.

'When did it happen? When did you meet her, Mikey?'

'When did I meet Sarah?'

'Yes, her! Who do you think I mean? Don't make me say her name!'

'A while ago. No. That's not quite true. A few days ago. I don't know. I can't really remember. I'm sorry, Tabbie. I didn't know this was going to happen.'

'Have you – oh god, Michael! – have you had sex with her?'

'No. Of course not.'

'Then how do you know she's the one? How do you know you like her more than me?'

'I… I don't know. It's just – well, it's like I've crossed a bridge. It's like I've spent all my life walking up to this bridge, and now I've crossed it. It's like I'm in a different country now, and I've got to write you a letter to say that I haven't got the money for a flight home.'

'But we had so much ahead of us, Michael! So much we haven't done yet! I've saved so much for you! You can't just walk away across some bloody bridge!'

'I'm sorry, Tabbie. I don't know what it is. It just happened out of the blue. Crash, bang – and everything's changed.'

'Everything? Oh, god, Michael…'

Clutching at his sleeve Tabitha began to sob. She seemed younger and more vulnerable in that moment than he had ever imagined her. He wanted to carry her to the bed and kiss away her tears and tuck her up to sleep with her favourite toy. 'I'm sorry, Tabbie,' he said.

And he was sorry. As sorry as he could possibly be, sated from sex with someone else.

'But what's so special about her?' she had cried. 'How can you throw so much away?'

'I don't think I knew there was that much to throw away… I don't think I was convinced we really had a future…'

'But we were going to get married, Mikey!'

Had she believed that until then?

'Goodbye, Tabitha.'

And that was another funny thing: something that puzzled him even now. One minute they were in love, the next they were not even friends. Whatever it had been in each other that he and Tabitha thought they had loved had vanished instantaneously, as invisible as the flames of a burning car in the brilliant sunlight of the Gaza Strip.

He had never seen Tabitha again, though he thought of her sometimes. He wondered, now and then, what she was doing.

He had never tried to contact her. She had never contacted him.

With Sarah there had been no war, not at the beginning, no unspoken treaties or secret pacts, no initial skirmish, no negotiated stand. There had never been any deployed barbed wire or toiling trench warfare. They were in bed together an hour after they met – a bed that until quite recently they had never really left. They were friends and lovers from the very start: through the easy days and through the cancer days. The sort of lovers who attracted the amused glances of waiters in restaurants as they sat, their hands clasped across the table, placing their orders and deciding what they should share. The sort of friends who held hands when they were hiking in the middle of nowhere, three-quarters lost on some mountainside in the Alps.

When had they been most in love? If he had to choose a time, he would probably choose the days when he used to pick her up from work, when he was still laying carpets, before he had got into phones and made them both rich. Sitting alone in the lounge, after cutting his mother off on the phone, he remembered driving Sarah into the countryside around London, treating the company van like a rally car. They drove out to the Banham estate where you could park unwatched amongst the trees, then tumbled into the back amongst the scraps of underlay and offcuts, half undressing one another. In seconds her muscular legs were wrapped around his hips, her heels digging into his calves. During those early days she had almost frightened him with her ferocity. He almost recoiled against the tin walls of the van as she bit and scratched at him, forcing him onto his back and holding him down, pounding at him with her hard, bony pelvis. Neither of them spoke during their love-making. They just worked away furiously like farm labourers making for lunchtime. No girl had ever been like this for him. Afterwards they talked for what seemed like hours, intimate and close, with him still inside her, enmeshed as the interlocking gears of a threshing machine.

Then they'd laughed, pulled on their clothes, and chattered all the way back to Ealing. He had wondered what she must have smelled like, sitting at her desk after that – earthy and sweet, with a hint of rubber underlay about her, of newly cut carpet. And he'd found himself consumed with jealousy at the notion of anyone catching even a hint of that sweet smell. He had been jealous, even in those early days, at the thought of someone, anyone, having the slightest vicarious pleasure of guessing what they had been doing in their endless-seeming lunchbreak.

Michael had always been jealous with Sarah. He was jealous still: hoarding the moments of their time together like jewels, seeing her time with others as something stolen, something of his.

Pushing the phone aside he stood up, walked into the kitchen, found his diary on the table, shoved it into the inner pocket of his suit. *I'm a silly, smitten, stupid, jealous husband. I always have been. I always will be.* Jealous at the thought of someone taking what he no longer had, of someone else coming to love Sarah's high cheekbones and thin legs and the bouncing brown bob of her hair which she had kept short since the chemotherapy.

Even now, standing in this empty house, he wanted to smell her, to smell what slight trace of his wife might linger here, to inhale *sarah* and imagine that he was pressing his head deep between her thighs.

He trembled with longing, with loss. If only she were here, right now, in this instant... the Sarah she used to be. He wanted her more than anything in the world. He wanted to pull down her knickers and taste her vulva. He wanted to push himself into her, push himself deep in, all of himself, until there was nothing of Michael Germain left, until he had fused with her in a process of unbirth, had returned to the womb and had been absorbed. He wanted to shut down his mind and become no more than a small part of Sarah, something she could never ever lose or abandon or leave behind.

There wouldn't be questions then, unanswered and unanswerable, like why the rich always felt they deserved to be rich and the poor always thought they deserved something better, or how on earth anyone could do anything but drown in the modern plague of opinion and information…

Deep in Sarah's infertile womb Michael imagined there had only ever been – would only ever be – utter, impregnable peace.

## Chapter Four

'Here it comes. Late as always.'

'Yes, but only by a minute or so.'

Jane picked up her travelling bag, glanced at her friend – and thought to herself that with one small push it could all be over. But who would push whom, she wondered – and, in the ensuing struggle, which of them would fall? She hardly cared. The journey they were making that day was very different from any journey she had ever made before. It was a journey towards change, a journey between two continents whose massive tectonic drift would make any return impossible, a journey to her son. And yet she felt uplifted as the train, the 16:01 from Chippenham to Bristol, growled into the station. She was being selfless, she thought. She was putting Michael's interests first. It was something she was unused to.

She clambered aboard with Mildred at her heels, selected a table where they could sit opposite one another, and laid out a handful of biscuits wrapped in clingfilm and a flask of peppermint tea. 'Everything's going well,' she said as she poured tea into the small china cups that Mildred proudly retrieved from her bag.

Mildred's expression was wary, as if the train were a predator into whose stomach they had been unwittingly drawn... 'Going well?' she asked. 'Compared with what?'

'Compared to the last time we travelled by train...'

'Anything would be better than our last journey. What was it, Jane? Two hours waiting for the train to arrive and then missing our station at the other end?'

'We didn't quite miss our station.'

'Only because you hit the emergency button.'

'I hit the emergency button because I had to. I've never allowed myself to miss a stop in my life. And no one minded. The guard was very sweet about it.'

'You didn't see the face he made behind your back.'

'He was a very nice man. I remember distinctly.'

'That's memory for you...'

*to the bridge*

'Well, this guard is different. I caught a glimpse of him when we got on. He has a very kind face, Millie dear, not unlike yours. Like a Pekinese.'

'He didn't speak to you, I don't suppose.'

'Why should he have?'

'Then let's not pre-judge the case.'

'Heads down,' Mildred said a few minutes later. 'Your Pekinese is on his way.'

The two women fixed their gaze through the window, taking in for the first time the passing landscape: harvested fields, the sparse hedgerows, the clusters of trees surrounding the mounds of iron-age forts.

'Tickets from Birmingham and Chippenham, please.'

Mildred pushed her ticket across the white table top. The guard picked it up – scrutinised it as if it were a border pass presented by someone with terrorist intent – then handed it back to Mildred, shaking his head.

'And your ticket, madam?' he said to Jane.

'If there's something wrong with hers, there's something wrong with mine.' Jane lifted her handbag onto her lap and began to scrabble within it. Why should she hurry? Why should she simplify the lives of the pen-pushers and stamp collectors of the world? At last she extracted a rather crumpled ticket and held it out to the guard. Taking it, he again shook his head. He was more a bulldog, she decided, than a Pekinese.

'Your tickets are Supersaver Returns,' he said.

'Super whats?'

'Supersaver Returns,' said the guard.

'I think we are in a foreign country,' Jane said to Mildred. 'Do you understand him?'

'What is the significance of a Supersaver Return?' Mildred asked.

'Its significance, madam, is that your tickets are not valid on this service.'

Jane stared hard into the man's eyes. 'Of course our tickets are valid. We only just bought them.'

'I am afraid they're invalid, nonetheless, madam. Saver Returns, Away Days and Supersaver Returns are not valid on this service between the times of four p.m. and seven p.m.'

'We boarded before four.'

25

'I am afraid not, madam. This train arrived at Chippenham for boarding at four oh one.' The guard fumbled at the machine hanging at his side. Unexpectedly silently – it should have whirred, Jane thought – the device performed some abstruse calculation. 'That will be an additional six pounds fifty-five pence, madam.'

'Each?'

Sensing payment, the guard's wrinkles smoothed. 'Six pounds fifty-five pence each, madam.'

'But the train only left after four because it was late!'

'Just cough up, Jane,' Mildred said. 'He's only doing his job.'

Jane expected absolute loyalty in her friends. Absolute loyalty and absolute courage. Betrayed, she said, 'That's always been your problem, Mildred. You won't stand up for your principles.'

'Dear, I have no principles to stand up for. That's what makes me a decent human being. Now cough up and shut up.'

The guard leant forward. His wrinkles multiplied. His eye teeth twinkled. 'Hurrmph,' he growled.

'My dear man,' Jane reasoned. 'Surely we can come to an amicable agreement? Charging us for a discrepancy of a few minutes is nothing less than criminal... How about three pounds?'

'Jane!'

'No, Mildred. This man is not an automaton. I am sure his job allows him discretion.' She smiled at the guard. 'Am I right? Or have you been reduced to following orders like a prison guard in a concentration camp?'

A Rottweiller now, the man's cheeks flapped. 'Six pounds fifty-five pence, please, madam.'

'Well, I don't have it.'

'Just pay him, Jane.'

'Can't pay, won't pay.'

Raising his eyes, the guard turned to Mildred. 'Now, madam. Perhaps you, at least, will pay the correct fare.'

'I can't pay if she won't... She would never forgive me... Jane, you simply have to pay!'

'Collaborator,' Jane said.

*to the bridge*

The guard glowered at the two women for a moment. He opened his mouth as if about to say something – something profoundly rude, Jane hoped – then shrugged and turned away. 'The revenue officers at Bristol Temple Meads will see to your problem, ladies. Enjoy your journey – but please have your tickets and money ready on arrival.'

Mildred and Jane crept through Bristol Temple Meads train station like escaped convicts – managed to get past the barriers without the discrepancy in their tickets being noticed – and fell into their taxi with sighs of relief.

The driver fired his vehicle into life. 'And where can I take you, my dears?'

'59 Sylvia Avenue – and we are not your dears!' Jane snapped.

'59 Sylvia Avenue, BS4. Right you are. Have you been to Perrett's Park before, ladies?'

Jane felt that question like a stab to the heart. How long had it been since she last visited? Two years? Three? She had abandoned her son to the care and the cruelty of another woman. How had she allowed herself to do that? How long had she intended to let such a situation continue?

They climbed out of the taxi to stand before a pretty Victorian terrace with curving steps leading from the street to arched and tiled porches and an abundance of stained glass.

Number 59, Michael's house, was well kept. The small front garden hoarded terracotta pots in a multitude of shapes and sizes, each overflowing with plants, some still in autumn flower. Lights were on in the windows.

Seeing Mildred stoop to pick up her travel bag, Jane reached out and gripped her arm.

'No…. Wait.' Jane studied the familiar house to check if anyone had seen them. 'I don't think I'm ready to confront the heathens. I have the feeling that if we go in now we'll end up in their cooking pots.'

'Well, you've not exactly been invited.'

'It's not that, Millie dear. It's just that I've never done it this way round before – going to Michael in his time of need. It's always been the other way around. He's always come to me.'

'You came to see him when Sarah was ill.'

*to the bridge*

'There was nothing else we could do. Visiting them in hospital wasn't optional; it was duty. This is different.'

Jane drew her friend away from the house. They crossed the road and stepped into Perrett's Park. The park fell away in a green sweep to the playground far below. Jane gazed out over the city. She needed time to compose herself. She needed time to assess who she was meant to be in this strange new adventure.

A lifetime in art had not prepared her for the role of missionary. She didn't know if a missionary's smug conceit was the uniform she wanted to wear.

## Chapter Five

Earlier that week Michael had dragged Sarah out to the park. Too much of what was going on was going on inside his head. He wanted to get it out. He wanted some sort of confrontation.

Perhaps he wanted catharsis.

Perhaps he simply wanted to connect.

'Let's go for a walk,' he said. 'Around the Perrett.'

Sarah allowed him a half-smile. 'Okay.'

She took her time finding her shoes, digging out a scarf. He watched her as if from a distance, thinking how beautiful she was. Although it wasn't cold she chose her mohair coat, wrapping it tightly around her. He thought she seemed distracted, as if her mind were on other things. Was she thinking about another man, he wondered? Or about the man she had hoped Michael would become?

They crossed the road into Perrett's Park. Everything was autumn. An early wind had cast leaves at random across the lawns. The air smelled of damp grass and car exhaust and soil. Michael walked at Sarah's side for a while without talking. They had always held hands when they walked together. He reached out now and took her hand, holding it as a father might hold a child's on a cliff-top hike. As they followed the edge of the park Michael was unable to hide from himself how unresponsive her hand was in his. Their skin touched but there was no transfer of warmth or emotion, no reaffirmation of affection or love. A tremor of fear ran through him. He imagined he was seeing the future – a future he could not bear. After a while he opened his hand. Sarah's fingers slipped from his. He walked ahead, towards the corner of the park, glanced back.

What little light the day had stolen from the sun seemed to gather about Sarah, binding her in a halo of warmth. Michael thought she seemed younger in that light, as if the fear she had been living with for so long was at last falling away. She seemed to have returned to a past summer, one to which Michael would forever be denied.

*to the bridge*

Feeling his throat constrict, he stepped towards her. He said, 'Sarah, we can't go on pretending nothing has changed.' There was a breeze from somewhere; his eyes began to smart. 'I feel... Sarah... I feel as if you don't love me anymore.'

Sarah turned away from him, looking out across the city. 'Don't say that.' She pushed her hands deep into her pockets. The summer he had seen surround her a moment before had gone. Her face was pinched against a self-inflicted cold. 'Of course I love you. But it's not about love, is it? It's about sex. You just don't want to believe that I can love you without having to jump into bed every five minutes.'

'Every five minutes? Every five weeks would be nice.'

'That's not the point, Michael.'

'But we don't even touch. We don't kiss or hug. How can we go on like this? How can I act as if everything's the same?'

'You can try for a bit. You haven't tried very hard.'

'I've tried for two years, Sarah. That's not just a bit. That's an age. I want to know when it will end. I want to know when we can just be ordinary again.'

'I wish I could tell you, Michael. I really wish I could tell you, but how can I? God hasn't given me a window into the future. Do you think my sexuality has a timetable that I can just refer to and there's the answer?'

'I don't want a timetable. All I want is something to pin my hopes on.'

'Oh, god, Michael! How can I know when I'll feel differently? It could be tomorrow. It could be next year.'

'It could be never.'

'You're making me hope it's never, the pressure you're putting me under...'

Michael kicked at the edge of the pavement where it was beginning to decay. Everything in Britain was beginning to decay. It was the nature of entropy. 'I might as well be your brother,' he said. 'Or just a friend sharing your house.'

'In bed with me?' She turned away. Michael felt the air between them freeze in place.

A man and a woman walked past, on their way to the city centre. They were very young, holding hands, their sexuality almost tangible between them. The girl's skirt caught tautly at her thighs with each stride. Michael watched the swaying of the fabric, the strong, confident movement of her legs. Longing stabbed through him like the pin that stabs a butterfly to the naturalist's board.

Extinction was breathing down his neck. Sarah noticed his gaze. She smiled coldly.

'Anyone would do, wouldn't they? Men are like that about sex...'

'No. No one else would do. You know that.'

'I don't believe you.'

She began to walk back towards the house. 'I'm hungry. You can cook me supper if you love me so much.'

'And what do I get in return?'

Lying beside her that night, how he regretted that false, foolish question... It had sounded as if he were turning their sexuality into a business transaction. Tit for tat. A return on his investment. And it wasn't just sex he wanted. Sarah was wrong about that. It was everything that sex said about the present, its affirmation of the future, everything it said about what they had left behind them in the past.

Sarah had said as they were falling asleep, 'Please don't touch me.'

Not even touch.

Those words hadn't been new. They hadn't surprised him. Yet they had jolted him awake like an electric current leaping through his flesh.

*Please don't touch me.*

This was what had become of their love.

He thought he detected a shudder as he put his hand against her back. He read it first as a shudder in himself. A shudder at the enormity of his loss, at the totality of her closure....

But it was her shudder, not his.

It held inescapable meaning: that he was shut out, not just from between her legs but from her soul and her heart.

Their giggling fumblings in the back of the carpet van were nothing now. Their long slow love-making in unnumbered beds on unnumbered holidays in Italy or Greece was nothing now. Those events had no continuity. They had no future. She had flung them like so much shrapnel into the dead maw of unreflective time.

*to the bridge*

He awoke before dawn the next morning feeling as if he had not slept at all but had spent the whole night working out the answer to a question he had already forgotten.

It was too early to get up, yet he was too restless to sleep. He walked around the bed, knelt down like a supplicant to look into Sarah's sleeping face. Why live together? Why not just visit every now and then for afternoon tea? The pale lines of her eye lashes lay still, undreaming. Her breathing was soft and steady. He saw in her face the face of the girl she once had been, as he first saw her on the Ealing train, as the girl who had slept four thousand nights in his bed, who had grown twelve years older in his care. The one who no longer loved him.

Her beauty was like the stigmata of Christ. The more he looked at it, the more he bled. He was bleeding now, kneeling there, a steady stream of blood pouring down his cheeks.

*No wonder she no longer loves me, with these weakling's tears streaming down my face.*

He dressed. Left the house. He didn't take much. A little money; his diary; a pen. He might want to write something, he thought. The lyrics of a song. A confession, perhaps. His time for confession would soon be over.

It was early still. The sky was clear. The day was filling up with light.

He made his way down through Perrett's Park then on to the roundabout on St John's Lane. He walked along the side of Victoria Park with its skeletal trees and lonely basketball stand, crossed the iron bridge over the Avon. The narrow river boiled between exposed mud flats, grey-green with the agricultural runoff it was carrying to the sea. He walked on, along the far side of the uneasy water towards the docks, passing a few people, not many, but turning his face away from them as he passed. He didn't want anyone to see the wounds his eyes had become. Vulnerability had infected him like a disease. *The tide needs to be higher,* he thought. *I'd better take my time.* He took his time, walking slowly, feeling that the world was drawing in around him, his vision narrowing, the people and places that he passed blurring into the edges of an alternative dimension. *I am no longer a part of this world. I have already begun to leave it behind.*

He had been walking for maybe an hour when he paused, trying to work out exactly where he was. Beside him iron railings defended a small, three foot garden. Above the garden the velvet-curtained home of a doctor or lawyer raised its Georgian brows. The tunnel of his decreasing vision allowed him to take in the green front door, the leonine door knocker, the large but secretive letter box. The houses to either side, the parked, upholstered cars, all seemed out of focus. The fog that clouded his vision even extended inwards. Even the questions he had been hanging onto – the questions that underlined the fracturing of the meaning of life – even these were fading away.

*Why do anything? What is the point of it all? Why are we here…?*
*They were such shallow questions. Why even ask?*

The lawyer's door opened.

'Can I help you?'

Michael couldn't look up. Eye contact would feel like an infringement of his soul. He turned, nearly tripped over himself, stumbled on up the gentle slope of the road.

'Are you alright?' the house owner called out behind him.

*Am I alright?*

Mildred would one day read in Michael's diary:

> You are driven to suicide by the closing down of all other options – including the option of staying as you are.

It was still early. He thought it must be around eight-thirty in the morning. People were going to work. The traffic throbbed like a distant heart. He was floating down a narrow tunnel, a stricture of perception, red-walled, opaque, an urban fallopian tube that expelled him into a square – gardens around the edges, a statue of someone long dead erected at its centre. He walked to a bench – at first hardly aware that someone was already seated at one end. He sat down, as far as possible from its prior occupant. The man already seated cleared his throat. He had shifted slightly, turning towards Michael. Michael kept his gaze fixed on his hands: hands that were no longer allowed to touch, that were no longer allowed to bring another person's flesh to life, that could neither recreate love nor inspire passion. They might as well be the hands of a ghost. He scrutinised the wedding ring on his forefinger. His father, Roger, on one of his increasingly brief incursions into

Michael's life, had said, 'Guard that ring well, Mikey. It starts off on your finger and ends up through your nose...'

Christ... it hadn't been his nose it had ended up on. If only it could have been – with Sarah still dragging him after her wherever it was that she was going. He would have followed her willingly, to the slaughterhouse or beyond, snorting, chomping, wagging his tightly curled tail.

No. His wedding ring had ended, taut as an assassin's garrotte, around the base of his penis: killing the masculine flow of his life.

'Excuse me,' said the man on the bench beside him. 'Do you know Bristol well?'

Michael looked up at the buildings beyond the statue. Bristol? He knew Bristol like the back of his hand. Yet the back of his hand was unrecognisable. It was the hand of someone he was in the process of leaving behind.

The stranger was waiting for an answer. Michael sat very still. If he pretended that no one was talking to him, perhaps no one would.

'I'm sorry.' The stranger shifted closer. 'Do you know Bristol at all, I wonder?'

At last Michael looked up. His new friend was middle-aged. He had the professional smile of a salesman. He was dressed in trainers, slacks, a blue sports vest. He was handsome with a hint of weakness. Middle-aged with a hint of grey.

Michael said, 'I don't know anywhere as well as I thought.'

'I'm not from here, you see,' the man said. 'I think I'm rather lost.'

'I see,' Michael said. He kept his gaze fixed on his hands.

'I'm from Victoria Island, in Canada. Have you been there? Oddly enough, it's a lot like this. It's beautiful, in the same old fashioned sort of way.'

*Go away,* Michael thought. *Leave me alone.*

'They call it the English Riviera. I'm over here to visit with my brother. He's a lawyer here in Bristol, you know. Calls himself a barrister. He has a flat above a law firm in, get this, "Clifton Village". He's working right now so I'm out exploring the territory.'

The man's accent was consistent with his clothes. His appearance matched his words. Registering the authenticity of his unwanted companion, Michael felt himself relax. A favour was not about to be asked, it seemed, or money begged.

*to the bridge*

'I've gotten myself lost. I'm looking for Kingdom Brunel's bridge. Do you know it?'

'No.' Michael reversed his hands, gazing intently at his palms. They were weak hands: the hands of someone whose personal space could easily be invaded by strangers. He had not known how weak they were. He had thought he was stronger. Conceding defeat, he said, 'You mean Clifton Suspension Bridge.'

'That's it.'

'It's not very far from here.'

'Can you direct me? Brunel was a remarkable man. Did you know he also built the Guadalupe Canal?'

A courteous English gentleman took control of Michael's lungs and lips and tongue: 'I'm going there,' he said. 'I'll show you the way.'

Inside himself he said: Leave me alone.

'Kind of you.' The man considered the offer. He scrutinised Michael for a moment; clearly thought the better of taking him up on his proposal. 'But no. Thank you all the same. I'd better be heading back. Where is it from here, though?'

With a slight nod of his head, Michael indicated the road running along the edge of the park. 'Follow that road all the way along. It's signposted from the junction at the top of the hill.'

'I'll wander up there tomorrow, then.'

The Canadian was gazing closely at Michael. Michael felt his eyes upon him, intrusive as an unwanted touch. 'So tell me,' the man said. 'Where have you escaped from?'

'I'm sorry?'

'There's nothing to apologise for. Isn't that an English phrase? Where have you escaped from? What's your asylum? Who's holding you captive? It's as good a way as any to describe the imprisonment of employment. I myself have escaped from the A-One Insurance Company, Vancouver Island.'

'I haven't escaped from anywhere, I'm afraid.'

'That's not something I can easily believe. You haven't robbed me yet. I've come to recognise the warning signs of the United Kingdom's great unwashed. The begging with menaces; ears and lips and eyebrows like sieves.'

*to the bridge*

'I work for myself,' Michael said. 'Perhaps that's part of the problem. I'm too locked up within my own life. I've got no one to blame. I've nothing to escape from. It's my wife who's escaped. I'm the one who's left behind.'

He regretted his confession as soon as he had spoken – relieved almost immediately that there was no reaching out to console, no camp gesture overtly repressed. Just the hum of Clifton traffic, the sound of footsteps behind them in the park. The Canadian said, 'I thought it might be something like that. I knew something was wrong as soon as I saw you. I've got an eye for that sort of thing, my friend. When it's there I see it. My ma had it too. She could look right into the heart of a man and put her finger on the hurt. You've got it. The hurt. I saw that right away.' He leant back, his elbows taking ownership of the bench. He clearly had time to spare. He cleared his throat. He's about to make a speech, Michael thought. The tourist said, 'I should be able to recognise that sort of pain, you know. You see, I've been left behind, too.' He gazed at the statue in the centre of the square. 'Not once – I wish it had been. No: many times. It's a habit of mine. I've had three wives. It feels like more. And lady friends, too. How many have come and gone? I couldn't count them on three hands. And you know what – it's always me who's the sucker. I don't leave. I don't dump anyone. I've never in my life written a Dear John letter. Oh no. It's always my companion who goes and me who's left high and dry. Somehow I don't learn. I'm never ready for it. I'm always thinking, this is it. This is the relationship that's going to last forever. But no. The bed's empty. The car's gone. The alimony's halfway to the bank.' He stretched out his legs phlegmatically; crossed his ankles. 'I'm alone now, though. I've been alone a year. I've decided to stay alone awhile. I'm finding a little consolation in learning to be independent, in learning how to stand on my own two feet.'

'That doesn't seem much of a consolation to me,' Michael said.

The Canadian reached out. He put his hand on Michael's arm. 'What did your countryman say? "No man's an island"? Being alone doesn't mean you're really alone, friend. Just look around.'

He took his hand from Michael's arm, stood up. 'I'll be seeing you,' he said. 'Have courage. That's all you need. And don't go jumping off that bridge!'

*to the bridge*

He began to saunter away, then turned back for a final word. 'The way I see it, we men have to learn to live on our own for a while. If we can't put up with ourselves, why should anyone else want to?'

When he was sure the Canadian had gone Michael pushed himself up from the bench. Resentment had leavened his depression, but it was not something he was pleased with. The Canadian had left him off balance. Michael had shared an intimacy he had wanted to keep to himself. In a sense, he had allowed an infinitesimal part of Sarah to escape. Resentment drove him from the square, up Constitution Hill, then on toward the edge of Clifton Downs. He could see the bridge at last. Resentment and gloom carried him towards it. He didn't stop at the window of the brick shanty at the near-end of the bridge. He couldn't face another interruption – and why should he donate a few pennies to cross the bridge when he knew he would never reach the other side? *I have had enough of gestures that have no meaning.* Almost at once he found himself at the centre of a group of Japanese tourists, crowding the footpath and chattering loudly to one another between snapshots. This is Bristol, he thought, Japanese style. He pushed through them, walked to the middle of the bridge. Stopped.

The Canadian had said something about beauty – about how beautiful Clifton was. Even here, high above the gorge, Michael couldn't see the beauty. He couldn't lift his eyes to look. He leant against the balustrade, staring down. There was a narrow tunnel stretching out before him, leading nowhere. That was all he could see. Behind him cars sidled past one another like predatory insects in courtship, second-guessing which one would eat the other. Pedestrians like aimless greenfly drifted at the edges of his vision, insubstantial as ghosts.

His feet scrabbled at the wire mesh that protected the sides of the bridge as he clambered onto the balustrade. He struggled for a moment with his balance.

Now he could see a little further.

He was standing at the edge of a precipitous height. A terrible, frightening, agonising height – and for some reason the tide was still out.

Michael saw himself falling. He saw himself plunging into the olive-green mud.

He didn't like the idea of plunging into mud.

Of being trapped in mud.

He didn't like the idea of not being able to write in his diary about his journey from Perrett's Park to Clifton suspension bridge.

There was so much to write about, to think about, to understand.

'Fuck,' he whispered, teetering there upon the brink of silent nothingness. 'Fucking fuck.'

And he was dull, he thought. His senses were dull with care.

*I didn't want dullness.*

There was a wind, a slight breeze. Like a hand it reached for him – a guide who knew the pathway down the long narrow valley to the sea.

'It's wrong,' he whispered. 'This…'

And the tunnel in which he had found himself led down, down, into the guts of depression, where the questions at first seemed more and more important and then not important at all.

'What the fuck is this all for?'

Loveless and unloved, there were no answers. The question itself was a spent force.

He drew back from the wind.

'I told you I was fucked, mum,' he said.

He turned away from the great drop – jumped back down to the pavement. The bridge was swaying with a life of its own. He could feel its movement beneath him. A Japanese tourist had taken Michael's photograph and was now shoving her smartphone under his nose.

The dark dull pressure suppressing his consciousness eased. He had not been able to weep until then. Now he wept, strung up somewhere between self-loathing and self-pity. The tourist looked at the damp marks on her phone's screen with something approaching awe – as if divine coincidence had bestowed upon her the Turin shroud.

'Thank you!' she cried out as Michael turned to escape the sway of the bridge. 'Thank you very much!'

There was a tunnel leading from the bridge: it was the tunnel of his life. It led into Clifton, down through Clifton Village towards the centre of town, then on, all the way to Perrett's Park. He entered the mouth of the tunnel.

As though his feet were caked in river mud, he began his journey home.

## Chapter Six

'I suppose," said Jane, "that I expected Michael to marry a wife a little less ordinary.'

'I suppose you did,' said Mildred.

They were sitting together on a bench in Perrett's Park, their backs to Michael's house on Sylvia Avenue. The city of Bristol sprawled out before them like a submissive mongrel, its tower block legs in the air, the River Avon its dirty bedraggled tail.

Jane said, 'And I thought Michael would pick a career a little less mundane.'

'Great Expectations,' Mildred observed. 'And like the book it was all just fiction.'

'I was surprised when they moved into such a small and ordinary house. Surely with all their money... and Michael's art degree... Well, I expected that Michael's life would be... out of the ordinary. I thought he would be a bit more like his father.'

'Like Roger?'

'Yes.'

'Roger was a cunt. I thought you knew that, Jane. In this world success and worth are totally unconnected – I thought your husband had taught you that, at least. Oh, please... you're not playing with that necklace again, are you?'

Jane had her rosary in her fingers. She was searching, bead by bead, for strength. She ignored her friend. 'Ordinariness wasn't something I expected in my son. He had so much talent, so much promise – and now look.' Bleakness consumed her. 'A phone salesman,' she said.

'Someone has to sell phones,' Mildred said. 'That's what makes the economy work.'

'But Roger... was so good with words... and *his* father, Roger's father, was in the Oxford Book of Verse...'

'Michael keeps his diaries – though you might not want to call that writing, I suppose.'

'Diaries are a form of mental illness, Millie.'

Mildred folded her hands upon her lap. 'Is that why you came here? Because you're afraid that Michael might be – '

'Ill?'

'Yes.'

'Mentally ill?'

'It's a question.'

'No.' Jane stood up suddenly. She walked to the edge of the path. As if venturing into a foreign continent she stepped onto the grass, looking back at Mildred. 'No. I've never believed that. Is that what you think?'

'We are all human.'

'Would you include even Roger in that category? No... I was just a little afraid, after what Michael said on the phone this morning, that he might do something stupid.'

'Then we had better go in and make sure he's not going to embarrass you.'

'It's not about embarrassment – and for once in my life it's not about me.'

"You shock me, Jane – and perhaps even worry me a little."

Picking up their travel bags they made their way to the gap in the railings and stepped through into Sylvia Avenue. Jane hesitated at the bottom of the steps to Number 59.

'Marshal your troops, girl,' Mildred said quietly.

Jane climbed the steps, establishing their beachhead in front of the porch. Mildred brought up reinforcements at the rear. 'Go on, then.'

Jane pushed the white porcelain button. Inside, a shrill electric buzzer rang out. She listened out for movement, heard steps approaching, the door opened.

Michael's wife, Sarah, was tall, slender, poised, unashamed of a contradictory chest. Her hair was far too short, in Jane's opinion, to be pretty; her face seemed a little pinched, and there were shadows beneath her eyes. Looking at her, Jane wondered what it was that Michael had found so enthralling in this young woman. Sarah was *ordinary*... an incidental, ordinary girlfriend whom Michael had forgotten to leave behind.

Whom he should long ago have left behind...

Sarah seemed neither pleased nor surprised to see them. Jane lifted up her travelling bag to emphasise that their visit was in earnest. Even then her son's long-time companion made no move to step aside and let them in.

'Hello, Jane. Hello, Aunt M.'

Jane peered past her. 'Is my son in?'

'Michael? No. He's been out for a while, I'm afraid.'

'Well...' Jane glanced at Mildred. 'Michael phoned me. This morning. He asked if I could come.'

'He didn't say anything to me. Was it important?'

'Of course it was important – or why would he phone me?'

Sarah's tone hardened. "Doesn't he phone when it's not important, too?' She deigned to notice Jane's baggage. 'I suppose you had better come in – though I can't say when he'll be home.'

Jane said, 'He knows I'm coming. He'll be home soon.'

Sarah led them into the hallway. A very ordinary entrance, Jane thought. Bare walls painted in neutral, pastel colours. Commonplace prints. She turned and waved for Mildred to follow, catching her friend's sympathetic smile to the young woman. Et tu, Brute, she thought.

She stepped into the lounge, turned to inspect the room. Even with conspirators on every side, God was here with her, she knew. God was on her side. Jesus was here beside her. Even without Mildred's support, the Son would give Jane the strength to go on. She could almost feel His hand upon her shoulder – guiding her, leading her to the sofa. Under divine instruction she folded her legs beneath her and made her peace with gravity.

This is *my* house, she thought. This is my house just as much as it is Sarah's. After all, it is Michael's house, and Michael is my son.

She sat silently in the lounge for a moment, avoiding Mildred's eyes when she joined her. A moment later Sarah came in with cups of tea on a tray. Then they sat there like three opposing forces massed upon a plain, each taking the measure of the other.

'So,' said Jane as Sarah sat down. 'What have you done with my son?'

Sarah's gaze was cold and adversarial. She handed her mother-in-law a cup of tea. 'You tell me,' she said.

## Chapter Seven

Again he awoke before dawn. It was a symptom of depression, to wake in the early hours, to lie there, restlessly struggling with his sleeplessness, strung out like a bridge over the gorge of his loveless life. He tossed and turned for half an hour or perhaps longer, trying to recapture sleep, then sat up with his arms around his knees and stared into the un-illuminating darkness of the bedroom.

He had been dreaming. Then he had woken with his mouth wide open as if preparing to howl out in rage or despair.

His dream was still there somewhere at the edge of memory. He sensed its presence, almost as if he were sensing the proximity of someone else's mind. Tread cautiously or it will be gone, he thought. Dreams do that. Striving not to be too alert – because being alert would dissolve the dream away – he seduced the remnants of his dream into view. He called softly to it; it meandered back into his consciousness in its own time.

He had dreamt he was a dog.

He had been driving with Sarah down the Wells Road, weaving in and out of the traffic with a complete disregard for pedestrians or other drivers. The body of the car around them was as ethereal as memory. They were two ghosts, devoid of material connection, stopping at traffic lights and pedestrian crossings only out of a shared sense of irony.

They drove past the ruins of the Wells Road cinema, its boarded-up façade redundant after the spread of the multiplex cinemas, past the Lion's football ground, used for years only by schools, and on, past fields and hedgerows and half-deserted villages all the way to the city of Wells. As they circled Wells Cathedral they heard voices singing, hoarse and cracked, like some distant barbarian army. Sarah was still with him at this point, seated next to him in the car – had been with him all this time, though he could just as well have been alone for all the good it did him. She was already cold, in his dream. In his dream, in a sense, she was already dead.

Near Stonehenge he saw the dogs. They came running through the farmlands parallel to the road. They were leaping the drainage ditches, the fences and hedges. He could see their teeth shining, their intelligent eyes. One or two of them lifted their heads to look inside the car. Behind them, bare-knuckled, shaking a granite fist at the sky, Stonehenge held its distance. Something clicked in Michael then. Something clicked or snapped. Something had changed in the car, too. Michael was no longer driving. Sarah was driving. She was driving fast. Cold but fast. Suddenly, without thinking, Michael threw open the car door. He glanced at Sarah, then leapt from the moving vehicle. He ran beside the car for a moment, looking in. He was hoping she would smile, would call him back – but she just kept on driving, very cold, very far away. What had he done, he wondered? How had he lost her? What had he done?

Until then he had been running on his back legs. The dog pack had drawn closer. They were nipping at one another, yelping and smiling, smiling not snarling, their teeth bared. Michael went down on all fours. In great lolloping strides he galloped at the pack's heels. The wind was in his hair. His knuckles were hard against the packed earth. A three-quarter moon already hung beneath the clouds, though it was still day. The dogs ran faster, faster than Sarah in her car, faster than all the cars on that naked stretch of road, faster than the wind. Soon they left the cars and their ghostly inhabitants behind. Michael opened his mouth to howl as he raced beside them, freed from the shackles of whatever it was that had bound him to Sarah, free at last of everything he had used to be, of his salesman life, of his failings and failures, of himself… He opened his mouth to howl – then closed it *snap*, rat trap quick, upon the unacceptable sound.

And here he was in his bedroom, sitting on the edge of the bed. Not running through fields, free as the wind, but sitting right here, trapped in a world that dreams could not change.

He stood up, walked to the bathroom, switched on the light.

*What had the dream told him?*

Sarah lifted her head from the pillow. 'What are you doing?'

'Nothing. Having a wee.'

Trapped – Michael thought – in the stone-solid rituals of their life. That was what his dream had meant.

He heard her roll over in the bed, away from the light, away from her husband. She was driving the ghost car into the distance. She was abandoning

Michael to the comradeship of his canine, cadaverous, appetite-driven friends, each a representation of himself.

Returning to the bedroom door, he stood there gazing down at her lovely shoulders, her shoulder blades and ribs. Everything she did, every movement she made, the way her arm was angled on the quilt, the visible strap of the slip she had begun to wear to bed, everything confirmed the closure of their love.

'I still love you,' she had said as they ate tea the previous night – as if picking up a conversation that needed concluding. 'How could I not love you after what we've been through? You are my best friend. There is no one else who comes near to how I feel about you. I just don't want physical contact right now. I can't do that at the moment.'

'For how long?'

'I don't know how long. How can I know what I'll feel in six months or a year? How can I answer that? It may be six months. It may be forever. This isn't about you. It's about me. About my needs. About the effects of the operation. About the effects of chemotherapy. About the effect of nearly dying – not once, but several times. You were there! You saw me. You held me. I've been re-born, Michael – you helped me to be reborn – and now I'm trying to work out what my new life means. Why can't you see that? I still love you, of course I do! But this has nothing to do with you. This isn't yours to own or understand. Not when it's still incomprehensible even to me...

'This is my puzzle, Michael. My problem...'

She had almost convinced him – for a while. But her chemotherapy had ended two years ago. Eighteen months ago she had returned to work. How could there be a puzzle which she hadn't yet solved? And could she really love someone whose touch made her skin crawl, whose kiss had become repulsive to her? Could she really love someone whom she couldn't bear to touch?

He turned away from her sleeping figure, from her isolating beauty, went back into the bathroom, stood before the mirror.

'I've been neutered,' he whispered. 'I could masturbate for an hour and not get an erection.' He reached down to check if his penis was still there – to *feel* if it was still there. He had been walking around for a year and a half – for two years – with a hollow space at his groin; a Not, a tangible nothingness, there between his legs. Put your hand anywhere near that vortex of absence and you might lose it at the wrist.

'You have emasculated me,' he whispered. 'I am a thing now. Not a man.' Un-manned, he turned and sat upon the toilet like a woman, letting his urine dribble soundlessly against the toilet bowl.

In his diary he wrote:

> I thought we were in love.
> I thought we would always be in love.
> I thought I was the miracle husband who dropped everything, put everything to one side, who made her illness possible to bear.

He was filled with loathing – for himself, for his life, for what he had become. He was filled with loathing for the fact that he was filled with loathing and not with joy. Sarah was alive. She had survived!

His self-indulgence and self-pity appalled him.

*Is there anyone in the world more despicable than this?*

'Where have you escaped from?' the Canadian had asked. Like a Castanedan apparition, the tourist had cut through all pretence.

> I am trapped,

> Mildred would one day read.

> Trapped.
> Trapped.
> Trapped.

'It's better than being *fucked*,' Mildred would say. 'Or, at least, I suppose it is...'

Michael was trapped – and the tourist from Vancouver's Little England had predicted his escape, or had at least cautioned him against it. Where can you go when there is nowhere to go?

You can go where nowhere is.

'Don't go jumping off that bridge,' the Canadian had said. He had meant, with a strange prescience, 'I know what you are going to do. Good luck, my friend... Good luck.'

*to the bridge*

Michael would write:

> I was trying to escape when I went to the bridge.
> I am still trying...

He dressed, left the house to its lonely inhabitant, set out across the park for the centre of the city and Clifton.

There was no Canadian this time in the small square in the centre of Clifton, just a park keeper in a yellow anorak moving amongst the flower beds.

Michael sank onto the bench that he had shared with the tourist. He didn't want to wait, but he could wait a little while. He had been too early last time. The tide had been out. This time he would get the timing right.

He looked down at his hands. Something he had discovered only recently: they were weak hands. He had a firm, strong handshake, a salesman's handshake... but weak hands. His palms ached with self-loathing and disgust. He splayed his fingers. Long, thin fingers. *Cut my hands off at the wrist and what would I be?* he wondered. *Stronger?*

He thought for the first time that he could almost understand compulsive hand-washing, could almost sympathise with the urge to wash and wash – that he might even like to give it a go. His self esteem had vanished into some remote outpost of his mind. He wished he could be washed *of himself*. 'Oh, god...' he murmured, 'All I want, all I really really want, is *out*...'

The park keeper, kneeling down beside a flowerbed a few yards away glanced up.

'I want out,' Michael said aloud. 'That's all. Is that so hard to understand?'

Giving an impression of carelessness, the park keeper straightened up and wandered over towards him.

'Are you okay?'

Michael couldn't look into her eyes. He shook his head. 'No,' he said. 'I don't think I am.'

'Do you have anywhere to go?'

'No,' Michael admitted. 'I've nowhere to go. Nowhere that I want to go to, at least. Nowhere except here.'

'I see.' The woman sat down beside him. She seemed as solid as a cargo ship in her yellow jacket, her Doc Martin shoes – but she was as calm as the ocean one mile down, her voice as imperturbable as the murmuring depths of the sea. 'So… you're on your way somewhere?'

'Yes… Aren't we all?' Too glib, he thought. Too glib for a strong man.

'No. Not all of us.'

Why shouldn't he tell her? 'I'm on my way to Clifton Suspension Bridge… to kill myself.' He glanced into her eyes, to see if she registered shock. There was no shock.

'To kill yourself… I see…' She didn't seem put out by his revelation. 'And you don't think that that's just a little bit selfish?'

'How can it be selfish?' *It's the opposite of selfish. It's the total annihilation of the self.*

'Do you have a family?'

Michael lied. 'No.'

There was truth in that.

'Parents?'

Again Michael lied. 'No.'

There was truth there, too.

'Then what about the rest of us? Don't we matter to you? Doesn't anyone matter to you?'

Michael felt himself becoming angry. It felt good to be angry. He wanted to be angry: tooth-grindingly enraged. He thought he had given up on anger long before – but anger was a positive feeling. A natural feeling. It made him feel almost strong.

'The rest of you?' he asked. 'Am I supposed to care about the rest of you? What was it Charles Bronson said in Deathwish? "I think you've mistaken me for someone who gives a fuck."'

'I'm not mistaking you for anyone, dear.' Her jacket shone a luminous yellow at his side, like a giant daisy or a sunflower. She went on, 'I'm talking about missed opportunities. I'm talking about who you could or should be taking with you.'

'I – I don't think I want to hear this.'

'You're selfish, then. Like I said. The least you can do, if you are going to commit suicide, is to take someone with you.'

*to the bridge*

He wished he hadn't spoken, hadn't provoked her. He was sitting next to a mad woman.

'Do you have someone in particular in mind?' he asked.

'It would be easy enough to choose... Someone wicked. Someone who deserves to die even more than you think you do. I could name one or two Latin American ex-presidents, I think. Or certain presidents of the United States. Or some ex-cabinet ministers now working in arms sales... Or a paedophile or a rapist... It's your last chance to make a worthless life worthwhile...'

'Mine or the rapist's?'

The woman seemed unruffled by the absurdity of their conversation. 'Yours,' she said.

Humour her, Michael thought. He asked, 'How about a criminally egotistical and acquisitive ex-Middle East peace envoy – if some suicide bomber hasn't already killed him?'

'He would be a good choice.'

'Or – or who was that awful sidekick of his? The egomaniac who went off to Europe?'

'Mendel?'

'Yes. Him.'

'Even better.'

'I'm not sure I could bear to spend so much time with someone so despicable.'

'You mean that long, final instant of your death – as the bomb explodes or the bullet hits?'

'It would be the rest of my life.'

As the park keeper walked away, Michael changed his mind. He wished he had told her everything. He wished he had told her about the life he had shared with Sarah before the cancer. About that eureka moment when he found the perfect phone for the perfect market niche. About how he was much, much richer than he looked – probably one of the people she despised. No mortgage, no loans, no debt, and savings that seemed to grow almost by themselves. And about the discovery of the tumour. About Sarah's operation and the months of chemotherapy. About how that made everything before it seem meaningless.

But why should a park keeper be interested in such trivia? Was he mistaking her for someone else, for someone who cared? She would be happy to see him walk away – especially if he served a purpose, furthering her political or ethical ends and not just his own...

In his diary Michael wrote:

> We are ricocheting off the walls of the world towards death.

And he would ask:

> What structure of belief can hinder my fall? What rational scaffolding of commandments or principles exists for me to catch hold of, or up which I might climb towards meaning and purpose?

It was almost lunchtime. On Constitution Hill, as he resumed his journey to the bridge, he found himself walking towards two business men, smart suits, silk ties. Michael coughed, his mouth filling with bile. They had those 'What can I sell you?' eyes with which he had grown so familiar – which probably mirrored his own. They had that 'How much money can you make me?' gait. Like Blair and Bush when they were in power, or Johnson and Trump: a comradeship of apes. They were smartphone and iPad carriers, infected with the plague which he had helped to spread.

Michael walked past them, shrugging off the past. He was escaping. He was the lucky one. They were just signposts pointing back through time to the life he was leaving behind.

When he arrived at the bridge the tide was in, the water was high, and the scene was set for the perfect fall. A touch of cloud had edged across the sky – but the day remained bright and balanced and pregnant with expectation and meaning.

Michael wondered if the wardens in the little brick shanty recognised him as he hurried past: the failed suicide from a few days before. At the middle of the bridge he scrambled onto the balustrade, feeling too old by far for this sort of ludicrous escapade.

Would they make a film about him, he wondered?

*The Great Escape.*

*to the bridge*

But the bridge was very high, higher than it had been the last time he stood there – and a policeman was striding from the far side of the bridge towards him.

'I can't do it,' he said to himself, balancing there, his arms outstretched like the wings of a flightless bird. 'At least, I can't do it without help.' There was a woman behind him, on the other side of the bridge, peering over the railing at the river far below. 'Excuse me?' he called out. 'Excuse me? Would you mind – ?'

The woman was small, frail, probably not of much use to herself or to anyone else. As she turned to stare at him he thought she might have been smiling wistfully to herself, perhaps exactly at her smallness and frailness, perhaps at her own inability to jump. 'Excuse me,' he called again. 'Can you help me? I need a push.'

There was something about the woman that reminded him of his mother: an edginess that hinted at fear. Standing there upon the brink he remembered thinking that his mother was afraid of him. Why else would you turn to God, except through fear?

*Mum ran straight from me into the arms of God,* he thought. *What sort of monster does that make me? Isn't it Satan's job – to make God necessary?*

The old woman – seeming stricken dumb – wouldn't help, of course. Why should she? What comparable favour had Michael ever done for her?

He looked down at the water far below.

'I'm still not ready,' he said. "I'm a million miles from being ready.'

His surrender was sudden and complete. He felt the will and the anger drain out of him. All he was trying to escape from was himself – and how did he know that he wouldn't be taking himself with him when he fell, down into a cataclysmic hell populated only by his own inescapable selfishness – just as the park keeper had said.

He turned around, waved back the policeman, jumped down to the tarmac.

He would go and see a doctor, he decided.

He would say to the doctor, 'Doctor, I need your help. I want to feel better about life. I feel worthless and trapped. I feel unwanted and unloved. I want to feel wanted and loved. I want to feel worthwhile and needed. But I don't think I ever will. I think all that is gone from me now…'

'There is a simple cure,' the doctor would answer. 'One I know you've already thought about: the destruction of the self. The rejection of identity. Death...'

But Michael would put his face in his hands and through trembling fingers mutter, 'Doctor – I'd like to take your advice, I really would... But tell me, tell me please – how will I know if the cure has worked?'

## Chapter Eight

Clutching her cup of tea like a drowning sailor clutching driftwood, Mildred sank into the comfortable sofa, gazing around at Michael's lounge. The room had something to say. Thinly slatted Venetian blinds; near empty bookcases; a single ornament on the mantelpiece. The room, or so it seemed to Mildred, informed all who entered it, 'We two have no time for trivia. We two are focussed on what is important. We are focussed on the real.'

'Such a sterile room!' Jane had whispered while Sarah was making the tea.

Mildred had dissembled. 'But nicer than it was, don't you think? A little less ordinary?'

'I only wish I could agree.'

'I'm only sad that the bookcase that you gave them has gone.'

'People don't read any more, Millie. Reading has become socially embarrassing, like smoking, or drinking too much. What a dry and sterile place the world will be without books!'

'I don't disagree.'

Jane had taken possession of the armchair in the bay window. Framed by the window she resembled a dowager queen holding court. No, Mildred thought – more imperious than mere royalty, she was like an empress visiting a long-since defeated colony, one that was increasingly unimportant in terms of culture or trade.

And she was making it plain to anyone who cared to notice that this was just a very small part of her empire.

*No wonder Sarah's hackles are up.*

Mildred said, when Sarah returned, 'We had such an interesting journey, Sarah! Eccentrics assailed us at every turn.'

Sarah lifted her cup of tea to her lips. Her movements were economical and her expression enigmatic, neither welcoming nor unwelcoming. Jane was certainly wrong to call her ordinary. *She is as imperious as Jane*, Mildred thought... *only thirty years younger.*

'That sounds ominous, Aunt M.'

'It was little short of a disaster,' Jane said.

'But an amusing disaster,' Mildred added. 'We had to slink through the train station in the hope of not being seen by the – what did the ticket inspector call them, Jane?"

"The Pekinese?"

"Yes, him. *Revenue officers,* he said. They'd be waiting for us. We hadn't paid the correct fare, you see.'

'We did,' Jane interrupted.

'Our tickets weren't valid for the train.'

'By one minute,' said Jane.

'That was very naughty of both of you,' said Sarah.

'Our tickets would have been valid,' Jane said, 'if the train hadn't been late. I find that unbelievable – that the ridiculous man should have asked us for more money. What is happening to our railways? How much must one pay to travel from A to B in this once welcoming land?'

'Michael and I hardly ever travel by train,' Sarah said. 'And when we do, Michael always insists on going First Class.'

'And then... then there was the taxi driver,' Mildred said.

'Yes,' agreed Jane. 'The taxi driver... I've never met such a terrible oaf.'

Sarah waited.

'He kept calling us *dears*, and he was thirty years our junior,' Jane said. 'What a preposterous individual! I could swear he was drunk.'

'You should report him,' Sarah said. She exchanged a glance with Mildred. 'I don't think a drunken taxi driver sounds very safe.'

*No, not ordinary,* Mildred thought. *I for one have never thought that. Whoever designed you, my dear, had the inspiration of a Michaelangelo – and Raphael's sense of the sublime. You are quietly and subtly beautiful and you know it.*

'Oh, I couldn't report him – what nonsense,' Jane contradicted. 'I liked him, drunk or not.' She put down her cup of tea, picked up her handbag, drew out the necklace of small wooden beads that she resorted to as a comforter.

*You're getting bored,* Mildred thought. *That's why you're playing with your rosary. You feel like making trouble. I can read the signs.*

*to the bridge*

Mildred forced the conversation on for half an hour – inconsequential, pleasant – all the while thinking how much she enjoyed being around younger people like Michael and Sarah, with their easy-going eloquence, their sparky intelligence.

*Jane and I spend too much time in our own company.* Out of the corner of her eye she watched as Jane grew steadily more restless.

'So my son hasn't left any sort of message? He didn't mention that he might be expecting me?'

Sarah was unflinching. 'I'm afraid not.'

'In that case I'm not sure what we should do.'

'Would you like to stay over? I'm sure Michael would be delighted to find you here in the morning.'

'Like waking into a nightmare,' Mildred said. 'Like sinking your teeth into an unripe cherry apple.'

At last Sarah smiled – and Mildred felt the tension in the room ease. Jane would never see how lovely her daughter-in-law was. She was too caught up in territorial warfare over Michael's affections. But outright hostilities needed two participants. Mildred smiled back at Sarah, admiring the poise which eight months of chemotherapy and several close skirmishes with neutropenic death had failed to demolish.

'I'll make up a bed, and get us some supper,' said Jane. 'You'll have to sleep down here, I'm afraid, Auntie.'

They ate a silent meal – silent, at least, of significance. Over salad bowls and pizza trays words drifted to and fro like airborne seeds, never settling, never taking root, holding only a faint promise of future meaning. At the beginning of the meal Jane had insisted on saying grace, with Mildred watching as Sarah watched Jane, half pleased at the young woman's unabashed gaze. *She has changed. No one can intimidate her anymore, not even a powerful old battle-axe like her mother-in-law.* Sarah had distanced herself from the world – and seemed to be inspecting it with immense detachment like a judge reflecting on a verdict she had made in error many years before.

All of that was hardly surprising, given what Sarah had been through in hospital and in the aftermath of her treatment. 'I'm beginning to take your health for granted, Sarah,' Mildred said. 'Are you still completely well?'

Sarah toyed with her salad of rocket, flat-leafed parsley, baby spinach leaf. 'I'm amazingly well, Aunt M, though I don't really believe that I can be. I keep thinking a new tumour will suddenly appear, or kidney failure suddenly set in. I often dream that I'm back in Ward 31, with the cannula in my wrist and chemicals dripping into my bloodstream – while the monitor ticks away beside me and the other patients snore behind their curtains. I don't think I'll ever feel completely safe again, Auntie, or entirely certain that I've escaped from all of that.'

Mildred found herself drawn into Sarah's world, seduced by her calm voice, her self-assurance, her level gaze. 'Why should you?' she asked. 'No one is ever truly safe, are they? An uneventful, unending future is just a myth that we all try to live by – but one that is periodically punctured by tragedy or illness or death. Luckily for you the human body's built-in redundancy allowed for your continued survival.'

'Nothing is redundant,' Jane said. 'Everything has a purpose.'

Sarah took her eyes from Mildred's. 'Only if you believe in God,' she said. 'Otherwise it all feels painfully arbitrary.'

Later, when they settled back in the lounge, Jane clearly became tired of the easy-going pleasantries. She asked in a querulous voice, 'How long has it been? Remind me, Sarah.'

'Since the chemotherapy?'

'No, not that! Since Michael abandoned his poor Israeli girl and the two of you hitched up? She was such a sweet girl, you know.'

Sarah's expression hardened, Mildred's painfully negotiated détente vanquished. 'That was more than twelve years ago. You might as well ask about Michael's girlfriends at primary school…'

'Girl*friend*, not *friends*. Michael didn't hop from girl to girl. He was always very constant. He lived with me until he was twenty-three. Twenty-three years, Sarah. That's a long time.'

In a clear demonstration of willpower Sarah drew back from open conflict. 'I wish I had known him then, as a boy.'

Mildred grimaced. 'No, you don't, dear,' she said. 'You wouldn't have liked him one little bit. He was obnoxious as a child. Most boys are.'

'Many, not most,' Jane corrected. 'Michael was nicer than most boys. He was sensitive. Not all boys like football and fighting, you know. Michael cleaved unto

*to the bridge*

his mother. We used to talk to one another about poetry and literature. He was closer to me than he was to his father, Roger. Mikey was a mother's boy. A feminine sort of boy.'

'Or thought he needed to make you think he was that sort of boy,' Mildred said. 'Mainly I remember him as a manipulative little monster who spent a good deal of time wheedling and whinging until he finally got his way... Not my favourite child... But he did improve, I'm glad to say.'

'He was a wonderful teenager,' Jane said. 'Idealistic. Full of hope and a sense of the potential perfection of the world. I was certain he was going to be a poet or a writer or something. Something grand.'

Mildred raised a doubtful, almost invisible eyebrow. 'That's how mothers tend to see their teenage boys. Bias would be understating the case.'

'I never thought for one moment that he might become something like a mobile phone salesman.'

'Not that that's such a bad thing,' added Mildred.

'Michael likes his work,' Sarah said. 'He enjoys being self-employed, managing his own time, being his own boss, making vast heaps of money.'

Jane looked down her nose. 'It will bore him eventually. Middle-age does funny things to a man. We women become more pragmatic – but men...'

'Pragmatic is a nice word,' Mildred said, 'though I'm not sure I would ever have described you in those terms, Jane.'

'Whose side are you on?'

'*Geriatric* would be a better choice of words, I think.'

'Speak for yourself!'

'Oh, if I'm speaking for myself I'd use the words "nine-tenths embalmed, largely decrepit, three-quarters senile and most definitely over-the-hill".'

Mildred was grateful – and pleased with herself – when Sarah's smile rekindled. It saddened her to see the lovely young woman trapped in such an inhospitable place.

'So where's that awful son of mine?' Jane demanded. 'Does he often vanish without warning? He never used to...'

'Often,' Sarah said. 'Sometimes we don't see each other for days – except when we are sleeping. But there's no reason why he shouldn't arrive home reasonably early tonight. I'm not aware of anything special happening.'

*to the bridge*

'He'll be networking,' Mildred said. 'Making friends and gaining influence.'

'How sordid,' Jane said.

'If he had his phone I'd give him a call,' Sarah said, 'but he doesn't carry one around with him anymore. He's started calling smartphones and the internet "the modern plague", just like you used to, Aunt M.'

'Then what's he doing selling the dreadful things?' Jane asked.

'Everyone has to work – at least nowadays.' Sarah stood up. 'And as I said, he may not like the system but he loves his work. He gets on well with people. He's good at communicating.' She glanced at Mildred. 'Time for bed, I think.'

After Sarah had ushered Jane in the direction of the spare bedroom, Mildred apologised. 'I'm sorry we've turned up like this, so unexpectedly.'

'There's not need to be sorry, Auntie. We always love to see you. I only wish I could say the same about…' She glanced at the door. 'It's like a military campaign when Jane visits. Michael should have warned me… would have warned me, probably, except for the fact that we aren't exactly talking at the moment.'

'I thought it must be something like that.'

'I thought when I got better everything would be fine… but it's not fine, not by a long way.'

'Oh, Sarah… getting on with the people you love, with the people who knew you as you were, was bound to be difficult after what you've been through. Serious illness changes people, you know. I've seen it before.'

Sarah smiled, a little forlornly. 'It's as if I'm suddenly unsure what to do with the rest of my life. It's as if the first half of my life was lived by someone else, someone I no longer know that well. Everything from before seems diminished, reduced, out-of-focus.'

'Death makes strangers of us all,' Mildred said.

'I should be filled with joy. I didn't die! Shouldn't that be enough to make anyone rejoice? But I don't feel joyful. I don't feel anything at all. I think I've lost the ability to feel. I'm floating on a sea of indifference and I can't see the shoreline and I'm not sure how much longer I want to stay afloat…'

Mildred took her hand. 'Oh, you'll survive,' she said. 'Why should you need shorelines when you have the intelligence and will and presence to swim forever across a sea of gold and light?'

57

*to the bridge*

'Oh, Auntie...' Sarah squeezed Mildred's hand, then let go and turned away. 'I hope you're right.'

Gazing at her, Mildred couldn't help but delight in their fleeting moment of intimacy. She loved Sarah – she always had. She loved all young women, couldn't avoid loving them when they were personable and attractive and knew their own minds. She saw in them the youth that she had so easily let slip away – not misspent but unspent; inhabited instead of lived.

*You have your life before you,* she thought. *Don't waste it on self-pity and introspection...*

When Sarah went to bed Mildred began to prowl. There was something about Michael and Sarah's home which she couldn't quite grasp – a sense in which it was more of an office or a shop than a home. Skirting the sofa bed, she scanned the shelves, taking in the scarcity of ornaments or books but the over-abundance of photographs of Sarah. The photographs, at least, were nice: Sarah happy and smiling in Westonbirt Arboretum; Sarah looking very young on the benches outside the Arnolfini Arts Centre in the centre of Bristol – Miller's bronze sailor pensive in the background. Sarah on a motorbike, a motorcycle helmet in the crook of her arm and her long legs bare. Sarah thin and pale, ravaged by chemotherapy, beautiful even without any hair.

The room beyond the lounge had once been the dining room. Now it was Michael's office. Mildred flicked the light on, gazing around her, letting everything sink in. Michael's business aesthetic matched his personal decor. The office was sparsely furnished, bare of ornaments, almost hostile in its nudity. To one side of the room there was a small conference table and chairs. A laptop with no visible printer or mouse lurked on the built-in desk in the corner beside the window. The only feature of the room that caught Mildred's attention were two posters on opposite walls, each displaying Michael's own make of phone: elegantly slim, its attractive user flatteringly reflected in the lens of the webcam. But neither these nor anything else in the room offered an insight into the working of Michael's mind. Impersonality, Mildred thought, personified Michael's office and the entire house. She sat down at the desk and began to work her way through the drawers – stopping abruptly when she thought she heard a creak on the stairs.

She waited a moment...

*Relax. Houses creak.*

58

*to the bridge*

...went on with her detective work.

In the drawers she found a miscellany of unreadable documents crammed with legalese; bundles of receipts scrawled over in biro; phone and network catalogues; catalogues of electronic parts. One drawer was locked, with no obvious key.

*Secretive,* Mildred thought. *Secretive – but dull.*

*Perhaps Jane is right,* she thought. *Perhaps Michael has become ordinary.*

She turned out the office lights, drifted into the kitchen.

The kitchen had the same air of almost superior detachment: uncluttered, unhomely, clean. There was a second telephone on an attractive dresser, wooden blinds hiding an original sash window, a pine table, hand-carved chairs. The dishwasher quietly hummed in holier-than-thou industry. On the sideboard next to a vase of flowers was one of Michael's diaries. He must have bought a job lot: the size and shape of a paperback, the cover an inscrutable black. Mildred picked the diary up. Where it fell open, she read:

> I am obsessed with breasts.

And further down the page:

> I must be reverting to childhood. I can think of nothing more imperative than burying my face in Sarah's breasts and lying there unmoving for hour after hour.

The diary was shut and back on the table. Mildred pulled her dressing gown tightly around her. Michael was secretive about his diaries... No wonder. But it was odd that he had left one lying around waiting to be read. She paused, then picked it up again. Taking the diary with her, she returned to the lounge and perched on the edge of the sofa bed. What this house really needed, she thought as she gazed around the room, was children. It was too clean. Too tidy. Too pedantically organised. She had seen this retentiveness in the homes of other childless couples – had seen a little of it even in herself.

And Michael and Sarah had no substitutes. No dogs or cats loved like children, given children's names and children's toys – no fish, birds, rabbits, tortoises – and she couldn't imagine either of them with giant teddy bears or cuddly toys.

Sarah, since surrogacy could never be totally excluded, had in a sense always been Michael's child. He had cradled her and nurtured her and worshipped her, even though someone so capable needed none of those things.

Perhaps that was the key to their new unhappiness.

Under the influence of drugs, drugs that attacked cancer cells and eradicated hair, Sarah had grown up.

She wasn't anyone's child anymore.

She was probably thinking – at last – of cutting the apron strings and leaving home.

Mildred dabbed some moisturiser onto her lips, then fished a clock out of her handbag and put it on the coffee table. She was old fashioned like that – using a clock instead of a phone. Turning out the lights, she climbed into bed with the aid of the strips of orange light falling through the blinds from the street lamp outside.

She imagined Sarah asleep upstairs, naked in her bed, long and slim as an arrow pointing towards the future, brittle as an arrow made of ice. She imagined Sarah suspended in an ocean of sleep, ice-bound, arctic, all judgement in abeyance, waiting for something inside her to speak out, to make its decision – waiting for the whisper of truth, for the immaterial, inaudible command:

*melt*

## Chapter Nine

Michael was on his back, staring into the emptiness of the sky.

For one night only he had become a member of the community of the homeless, sleeping on a bench.

*For one night only?*

The interwoven branches of plane trees, like blood vessels of a larger eye enclosing his own, interrupted the edges of his vision.

*Hasn't it been for a year at least? Or perhaps two?*

The sky was a fathomless blue, the blue of Sarah's eyes. Michael imagined for a moment that he had woken up to find himself looking out at the perfection of the sky through his wife's eyes.

Sarah…

…and Sarah's eyes.

Her eyes, lips, teeth, tongue.

He could almost feel her touch upon his skin, loving him still, their hearts and souls undivided as they had been, oh, not so very long ago… but the touch was just the breeze, caressing his skin, plucking at his clothes.

It was whispering to him, that soft, cold wind.

*I will make you naked, child… naked as a child.*

*I will make you child-light… lighter than a feather.*

*I will make you feather-light… lighter than the morning light.*

He pushed his hands deep into his pockets… shivered… He had been cold in the night – and glad that he was tired enough to sleep. Stirring once or twice, trembling, hugging his arms to his chest, he had sensed someone standing close beside him in the darkness, looking down into his face. But Michael had wanted no interruption to his misery, no compassion, no aggression, no interaction of any kind. He had rolled away and in an instant was once again fast asleep. This bench was his domain. No envious onlooker was entitled to any part of it.

Lying there now he smiled to himself – smiled for perhaps the first time in a week. The bench was not a bed to fight over, not in fact any sort of territory that anyone could wish to defend. Though the creeping night-wanderer might have

*to the bridge*

thought it was for sitting on, this was not in fact the case. It had been designed by a sadist with a hangover. Only someone buffered by the nervous system of a coelacanth could have found comfort in the curve of the sharp wooden slats. Only someone with a dangerously concave spine could have taken pleasure in the overhanging backrest.

This much had been obvious as soon as Michael occupied the bench the previous evening. He had tried lying on his back but that hadn't helped at all. The bench's designer – architect of train seats, racing saddles, shirt collars, airplane toilets – had been there before him. The bench was constructed so that any ordinary person, lying down, would find the edges of the planks digging into their calves. It was designed so that the hump in the middle would eventually roll its sleeping victim off the bench unless constant vigilance was maintained. Twisting and turning in search of its least uncomfortable position, Michael imagined its designer deriving undying pleasure in the success of his masterwork. He imagined the designer watching him, chuckling into his beard.

And someone had been there, watching him, motionless in the darkness beside the bench.

Gazing at the open sky, Michael's saw himself suspended high above the waters of the River Avon, the long green flanks of Clifton Gorge bracketing his consciousness, the wind running down the valley and plucking at the edges of the person he had become. He realised that he had achieved an unusual and profound lucidity.

These several, foolish journeys to Clifton Suspension Bridge had left him scarred. They had confirmed his impotence, rubber-stamping his inability to succeed. He was incapable of even the simple success of a death of his own choosing.

But now that had changed. His night upon the torturer's rack had given him something new.

Michael sat up, hunching his back to accommodate the architecture of the seat. On the bench opposite – which had clearly been designed by a more benevolent mind – another man lay sleeping. He was wrapped in warmer, more appropriate clothes: a long coat bulked out with several layers of clothing underneath; a woollen hat pulled down over his eyes, a rat-tailed scarf. His

*to the bridge*

heavily booted feet were thrust into a plastic bag; an undisciplined beard ambled across his chest.

Michael recognised his midnight guardian – the stranger who had been watching beside him as he slept.

The sun edged over the tops of the trees.

Traffic built up in the surrounding streets.

Michael felt a sense of comradeship and peace as he sat there, opposite his sleeping companion. It was the start of a beautiful day and Michael Germain was utterly empty of motive. He had drawn back once, twice, from the brink of death. He had looked down once, twice, and had been unable to see the water far below.

It was a kind of vertigo, he thought. Blindness induced by fear.

So much had changed...

His fear had vanished with the night.

A man wearing a blue waterproof walked past, rummaging in a sack of post. He wore sensible shoes, a baseball cap. Watching him, Michael expected him to stop, to look from one to the other of the benches' occupants and then push a letter into the hands of the snoring tramp. Michael could imagine what the letter would have said. It had been written by a terminally ill Canadian whose agent had sought out this poor, destitute man, here in this very park. The letter would detail an inheritance of wide estates, four rivers, a dam perpetrated by a family of beavers, three quarters of a forest.

It was the dying testament of the father who had abandoned Michael's companion as a child, and who had at last recognised the enormity of his loss.

As Michael's father never had.

Michael stood up, stretched, but no longer felt either stiff or cold.

He said to the sleeping tramp, 'You've missed the post,' then he followed the postman, carrier of a thousand bereavements, out of the park.

He had found a new resolve.

He had found, somewhere in the wasteland of dream, new answers to his questions.

He realised, for example, why so many people were unhappy despite being reminded with every evening news of the generosity of their condition in contrast to that of other people in other parts of the world.

*to the bridge*

He realised now why he felt unfulfilled despite having the wealth of twenty ancient kings.

His unhappiness was an attribute of the structure of his mind.

His mind was a mechanism made of pulleys and chains and spindles and cogs.

The mechanism had been wide open when he was born, had contained a million openings of all different apertures and shapes – but those spaces were now mostly closed. Schooling, conditioning, advertising, parenting, had all made sure of that.

Now only certain things could fit. Only limited interpretations of the world could slot into place – and the place into which they could slot would only confirm the truths that the structure had incorporated into its final unbending shape. In, through some twisted aperture, came Sarah's note, saying she was out. The note was turned and squeezed and crushed until finally it found a place upon a pre-prepared platform, Platform A, at the centre of his mind. There, its feather-light weight was just enough to send the wheels spinning and the chains rattling and the parsimonious Platform A plummeting down down deep down into the super-structure of depression upon which the whole construction now sat.

That was the way he was built.

He could see only darkness. The light of birth, dawn, spring, love, life, had dimmed into non-existence.

Well, it was time to dismantle the bars of the cage that had trapped him. It was time to blast a hole into the walls of the machine.

Pausing at a street crossing, he reached for his pencil and diary. He found a pencil in his pocket but no diary. He had left it behind him at the house. Why had he done that? he wondered. He put the pencil back in his pocket.

He knew exactly why.

He had left it behind him as a form of punishment, to rankle like a new kind of cancer at the core of Sarah's mind.

He had written:

> Why does one opinion matter more than any other? Amongst all this gossip and supposition, how on earth am I supposed to know what to believe?

And:

> How can anyone decide in this strange, absurd world what is right or what is wrong?

Well, he almost felt he had the answer there.

This world in which he found himself was polluted with interpretation, evaluation, assessment, belief. You could hardly think for other people's thoughts muscling their way into your mind. There were newspapers and television, hoardings and billboards, car stickers and signposts, radio and graffiti, voicemail and email, txt msgs and instagrams, Facebook, Twitter and WhatsApp. There were shopfronts and street vendors, mailshots and podcasts, countless thousand hardbacks and countless million paperbacks and a hundred million blogs published each year. There were a billion opinions in a million different guises, all of them colonising the landscape of the mind.

Other people's opinions, other people's minds: imperialistic; invidious; inescapable; unavoidable.

And which opinion should you choose?

Which side should you take?

*None.*

*None whatsoever.*

No, he was going to cleanse himself of the social babble. He was going to strip away the superficial. He was going to walk naked into the face of the real.

He took off his jacket, hung it on some railings as he passed.

A woman on the opposite pavement stopped to stare at him. He smiled – smiling was almost becoming a habit – walked on.

He had written:

> Why have I lost my sense of the beauty of the world? Why can't I see it any more? I used to see it. That perception of beauty was something I always used to have. Mum called it my 'poet's eye'. Like an artist's eye for shape and colour, I had an eye for the fabulousness of the world. Why have I lost it? Where has it gone?

His father, Roger, would have said that all Michael needed was a good fuck.

That had been his father's cure-all and salve: a good fuck.

It was a long time since Michael had felt the marvellous healing power of the entrenched cock.

Halfway up Constitution Hill he took off his shirt. The tall houses to either side looked down on him, unsurprised. A man was walking towards him. Michael recognised straight away that he had the plague. He knew the signs. Its most obvious symptom was the slight weight of a phone in the inside breast pocket, the black leech of a speaker in his ear. Its after-effect was to transform its host into a poorly-trained, loud and rude receptionist. Michael had been one of the plague's fervent distributors. He looked into the man's face. He was no longer afraid to meet his fellow pedestrians' eyes. Let them see the empty sockets that he now displayed, devoid of empathy or soul. He too had once had eyes. Prick him and did he not bleed?

Embarrassed at Michael's bare-faced arrogance the stranger fell silent for a moment, then resumed his self-proclaiming conversation as he walked past.

*I care nothing for you,* Michael thought. *I am transforming into something new. I will be as naked and vulnerable as a child.* He wished he could write that down. It would have looked good in his diary… but what was the use of a diary he would never again write in and never again read? Perhaps – if he had brought it with him – he could have snatched it from his pocket as he tumbled from the bridge and in a hasty scrawl written:

>I've made it!

Or just:

>I love you, Sarah.

Or simply,

>Yes!

And then, on impact, first with water as hard as a brick wall and then with a riverbed as soft as down, the diary would find itself submerged, first in water and then in mud, compressed by time – its ink replaced by iron ore, its cover infused with quartz.

Millennia would pass.

More millennia would pass.

Then in some strange and future time an alien race would discover the fossilised book. With magic like science they would decipher its crystalline words...

>Who am I?

>What am I?

>Why the fuck am I here?

He had left his shoes behind him somewhere. He was walking in his socks. Shopfronts filled with gifts for the well-heeled inspected him disdainfully. This was Bath stone Clifton, inhospitable to the tramp he had become. A woman ushered her children to the other side of the street as if he had the plague. He was cold, getting colder, but he felt that that was right. The real world, not the world of self-inflicted thought, was forcing its way into his mind. He wanted to feel his eyes – or what was left in the sockets of his eyes – forced wide by the cold clear light; he wanted to feel his skin flayed raw by the cold.

He was dismantling the machine.

He was going to let the light come shining through.

The road to the bridge lay before him. In the parkland leading to the Downs tall plane trees, and beech and oak, clung on to their last golden leaves, children they hated to release. A man with three pedigree dogs drew them back, as if Michael were an apparition even the dogs should not see. For a moment he was reminded of his dream, of the canine predator he had become. The northern tower of the bridge towered before him, its great wrought iron chains sweeping out across the gorge.

Though it was early, perhaps only seven-thirty, the bridge was busy, lines of cars halting at the toll machines then crawling beneath the uplifted barriers to cross the bridge. Anxious faces hovered above the steering wheels. They looked cold in their cars – colder than he was – the timid ghosts of other people's lives.

*to the bridge*

There were fewer pedestrians than the previous times he had come. A group of children were walking towards him, uniform in their uniforms but perfectly individual in their open shining faces.

*How I wish… How I wish that Sarah and I had had children…*

He wanted to become someone other than the person he had become.

He ran his fingers over the wire mesh that stopped birds from flying through the balustrades.

He wanted to be free from wire mesh and metal stanchions and wrought iron chains. He wanted to be free from emotional bondage, from a wife who no longer loved him, from the work that made his living, from the mother who formed his past, from the shape of things to come.

He wanted to be shapeless and formless and free.

He came to the centre of the bridge, its slight rise beneath his feet, its swooping, suspending chains as low as they could be. Standing there, he thought that by now he must be a familiar sight – but not without his trousers.

He was almost surprised no one was there expecting him. Did failed suicides not usually return?

He lowered his trousers and boxer shorts, stood there in nothing more than his socks. Four children stared at him wide-eyed, clutching their school bags. Michael imagined their delighted retelling of their adventure, later at school.

'There was a weirdo,' they would say. 'There was this weirdo on the bridge. You should have seen him. He took off all his clothes and – '

'Don't try this at home,' he said. He pulled off his socks. He felt a little bit like a fool. What would they make of him? How could they reconcile this with the repetitive daily cycle of their lives? He climbed onto the balustrade – it was easier barefoot than it had been in shoes – and looked out across the valley. The beautiful city of Bristol lay like a construction of salt and ice in the valley's cusp.

He had gotten it wrong before.

It was wrong to sink into oblivion filled with self-loathing and remorse.

He had gotten it wrong again.

It was wrong to leap into death like an animal, tearing itself free from the grip of a snare.

And he had got the tide wrong.

Now, everything was right.

The tide was in, the river was full, and a crisp, clear breeze was caressing the skin of his face, mapping out the territory of his senses of perception, tracing each single strand of hair upon his scalp.

'I love you, Sarah,' he had wanted to shout as he prepared to leap. Or, 'I forgive you, mum.'

Instead he just said, 'Third time lucky.'

Then he stepped out –

– and was in the air at last.

*to the bridge*

*to the bridge*

# Part Two
# Ways To Exist

*to the bridge*

## Chapter Ten

This

*to the bridge*



















                                        is

*to the bridge*

it

*to the bridge*

no tumbling
    chaotic
half-witted
   fumbled
      *descent into chaos*

     just…



                             ***this***.

*I am what I am*, Michael thinks, amazed that he is capable of thinking at all.
*I am what I am…*

*I –*

*I am this being, here, high above the River Avon, pinned to the sky, my gaze as intense and hungry as the beam of a laser, my gaze as intense as a laser stabbing outward across the landscape of buildings and bridges and docks –*
*Stabbing out across the landscape of Bristol in a desperate search for –*
*Hungrily, desperately, avidly seeking –*
*My gaze as caustic and searing and fervent as an acetylene torch in the hands of a torturer, hunting, seeking –*

For an instant – or for at least the smallest fraction of an instant – Michael Germain is not falling.

He is suspended a quarter of a metre above the level of the balustrade and almost a metre out into the open air.

Behind him, on his left, is the sandstone-clad outcrop that supports the tower on the Clifton side of the bridge. Behind him, on his right, is the abutment beneath Leigh Tower – with its complex of secret chambers and narrow tunnels through which a grown man would barely be able to crawl…

Whose kindergarten playground was this designed to be? Michael wonders.

Had the wonderful Isambard Brunel, in some dark but prescient corner of his soul, recognised that he would die long before the bridge would ever be completed?

Had he left behind this labyrinth as a mausoleum for his ghost?

Isambard Kingdom Brunel – wind-torn, beetle-browed, paternally-oppressed survivor – shivers into existence beside Michael as he hangs suspended above the gorge. The two of them linger there, side by side, neither supported, neither falling, both participating in an existential joke whose precise intention neither of them can quite discern – the engineer introspective, blind to the flung out angel's wings of the suspension bridge behind him, self-contained, preternaturally calm, Michael somehow hungry, somehow needy, suspended beyond the bridge's lip for just this fraction of an instant, his gaze reaching out, his soul reaching out, seeking, desperately searching –

*Am I – ?*

*Am I really here, suspended on a pillar of air that is exactly as long and as tall as the rest of my life?*
    *Christ…*
    *What a feeling…*
    *What a fantastic, terrifying, wonderful feeling!*

To the north side of the river, above the Clifton Gorge Hotel, a herring gull is hovering, its wings outstretched towards the horizon.

To the south of the river outcrops of granite and thickets of gorse clamber over one another's shoulders towards the brow of the hill.

The sky is as clear and perfect a blue as –

The sky, lovely, luminous, unfathomable, is as perfect a blue as –

*I –*

*I am what I am,* Michael thinks.
    *Or am I – ?*

Sound has stopped. Mid-arc, its invisible waves have been intercepted by Michael's leap. Sound has stopped like a broken-down train, stock-still dead in its tracks.

The traffic has stopped.

The wind has stopped.

The wind has stopped mid-puff, it's great billowing cheeks temporarily lulled.

Even Michael's heart has stopped.

In the moment that he leapt from the balustrade he had heard his heart pounding like a sledgehammer in his chest, pounding like the pistons of an engine whose boiler is about to burst. He had been sure in that instant that his heart was about to explode.

*to the bridge*

He had been certain that heart failure would kill him before he had fallen even half a metre.

Now he hears nothing.

The kettle drum beneath his ribs has stopped its beating.

The out-of-control steam engine has expired.

His heart has stopped.

*Her* heart has stopped.

He is searching –

In his diary he once wrote,

> There is nothing I can see that makes sense of what I see. Nothing I can say that makes sense.
>
> Nothing…
>
> …except your name.

Beyond the gull's wingtip the February sun hints of warmer days to come. Winter will pass. Spring is on the horizon, summer not far behind.

*Sarah?*

Amongst the gantries and docks, the marinas and locks he is searching for Sarah. For her lips, her eyes, her nose, her mouth.

For Sarah's stomach, her collar bone, her shoulders, her neck.

For the hollow at the base of her spine.

He is raking the landscape for some trace of their lives, for proof that they ever lived in this wonderful city, for evidence of his journeys to the hospital, of their journeys together to cafes, restaurants, supermarkets, swimming pools, for evidence of their trips to the Colston Hall, to St. George's Hall, to the Hippodrome, to the decaying cinema halfway down the Wells Road.

And Brunel, hanging there at his side, seems genuinely amused! He glances down towards the river, takes the cigar from his lips, inspects its sodden tip. He says, 'In your place, son, I'd build myself a ladder. A moving ladder powered by steam.' And the great engineer – paranoid, arrogant, brain-storming, chain-smoking product of his age – is laughing, despite the fact that he has long since found it difficult to breath.

Michael tries to laugh too. It comes to him as a blinding flash of light – a revelation.

There is ecstasy and joy in every aspect of life.

Even in loss and desolation and pain.

The bridge – Isambard Kingdom Brunel's bridge – is two hundred and fourteen metres wide.

Its towers are twenty-six metres high.

The roadway, tarmac'd now but once surfaced with wooden planks, is suspended seventy-five metres above the surface of the River Avon – or approximately that when the tide is in.

How the craftsmen must have toiled with their pulleys and ropes, their chisels and mallets, their hods and buckets dangerously overflowing with chippings or cement! How they must have cursed as they manoeuvred into place the Cornish sandstone blocks – or haplessly chiselled at the grey slabs of local Pennant stone!

Michael sees the men and boys working behind him now, scaling the slopes of the gorge for the penny-pinching pittance Isambard offers them, hauling baskets up the sides of the towers and yelling in triumph as they hammer home the red hot rivets of the chain.

He can smell the burning charcoal of the portable foundry, the acrid scent of chiselled stone, the sluggish waft of the river far below, the smell of sweat. He can feel, emanating from the bridge itself, the icy determination, the careless fatalism of its builders.

The bridge, after all, is not only Isambard Brunel's.

It is the creation of every man and boy who ever worked on its construction.

*Time* is behaving oddly.

It is not a phenomenon that Michael will ever have the time to describe.

He reaches for the diary in his breast pocket – then remembers that he is naked, his jacket abandoned on the railings of a house on Constitution Hill.

For a moment – for the barest fraction of a moment – he feels strangled by regret. If he had his diary, if he had a pen in his hand, he would have had the time to write:

> *I love you, Sarah.*  *I miss you, Sarah.*
> *I miss you.*  *I love you.*
> *I love you.*  *Christ, how I miss you.*

He'd have had the time to write the story of his life.

*Time* is behaving oddly.

For the brief flickering of an instant someone or something is allowing him all the time in the world.

Hyper-tensile time.

E-l-a-s-t-i-c time.

His fingertips burn with a sense of temporality, with a supernatural perception of time and space. All the moments that ever there were are compressed into this sub-second fragment of a particle of a moment, compact as an old-fashioned spherical grenade with a lit fuse smouldering at its lip. The whole thing, the entire world in fact, feels ready to explode.

*Sarah?*

Perpendicular to the sky, Michael is imbued with a sense of power over time.

His fingertips are like balloons, engorged with time, without the likelihood of deflating any time soon.

He is time's king. With a click of his fingers he can resurrect millennia. A summoning gesture, out across the Avon towards the tobacco warehouses at the head of the docks, and the long-dead workers come crowding to the warehouse gates, cloth capped van drivers hurrying to their vans to cart away the bales of tobacco.

*Carcinogens in, carcinogens out,* a child's voice begins to sing, bringing sound back to the city.

> *Carcinogens in, carcinogens out,*
> *Who knows what it's all about?*

Lord of space and time, Michael nods his chin towards the docks where the masts of the S. S. Great Britain reach up towards the sky. With a twitch of his eyebrow he resurrects the craftsmen working there.

They are lowering into place the wrought iron sheets of the hull…

What a stupendous idea!

What a ridiculous, mad-cap notion!

An iron ship that doesn't sink!

Michael keeps forgetting that he is naked.

It shouldn't be easy to forget that you undressed before of a crowd of school children as they crossed the suspension bridge, mouths agape.

Socks, shoes, trousers, shirt – nothing separates him from the fabric of the world. Bare-skinned and soul-naked, his consciousness mingles with all of time, with the future and the past. The detritus of his life is sleeping upon the river bank. His memories and dreams drift away amongst the moorings and the boats. The Lloyds building, the statue of Cary Grant outside the Exploratory, the funnels of Pero's Bridge, the tobacco factories, the Arnolfini, the Hippodrome, King's Square, Queen's Square, Prince Street, Prince Street Bridge – they are all places where Michael Germain is.

*This is my city. The city I love.*

Time has engraved his life upon the brick and concrete buildings, the tarmac'd roads, the pedestrian crossings and cycle ways, upon Brandon Hill, St. Michael's Hill, Windmill Hill and Three Mile Hill. His life is imprinted on glass and tile, on corrugated aluminium roofing, on old, black pitch. His life is a shallow ripple dancing over the brown river water and the oily docks. And it has direction, a barely visible trail that must be read backwards: leading up towards the bridge, leading along Clifton Down Road towards the gorge, slicing through Clifton Village, ascending Constitution Hill, meandering along the edge of the river, skirting Victoria Park, turning the corner by the old electrical appliance shop where St John's Lane becomes Saint Luke's Road, cutting across Perrett's Park – leading all the way from 59 Sylvia Avenue.

Number 59.

A quiet and sensible number for a quiet and sensible home.

He can see Sarah there – yes, he can see her at last! – waking up in their bed.

*to the bridge*

Michael shakes his head. Almost a metre out from the bridge and he is still rock steady, locked into position against the sky – but landscape and memory rattle like dice in the cavity of his skull.

Sarah pushes back the duvet and sits on the edge of the bed. The bed straddles with tower block legs the whole of the city. Time, energy, probability, space miscegenate, merge, intermingle, become one another.

The Dundry Hills, Upper Knowle, Three Mile Hill form a bowl around the heart of Bristol. Further away other hills emerge, green clad, escaping the city's grip. The city centre is in turmoil. The riots of 1831 still rage. Smoke from burning buildings lingers in the air. Slave-owning merchant princes peer out through leaded windows, weighing turnover against cost.

There are even places in this landscape that don't belong to Bristol. Over beyond the football ground Michael can see his Cheltenham primary school, his bed-sit in Forest Hill, his father's flat in Hackney. There are places here that aren't even places at all but are as tangible as Queen's Square or the tower blocks of Brandon Hill, like the memory of Aunt Mildred helping him dress for school while his mum sleeps in the next room, ill with flu. 'Come along, Mikey, dear. Don't make us late…'

Or the memory of his father chucking him under the chin and saying, 'Don't worry, little fellah – your mum will look after you… Your poor old pa's just a big waste of space, don't ya know? Your mum's already told you that, hasn't she? I bet she has. I bet she says that all the time.'

Michael's father Roger never speaks in his own voice – he is an actor and can never stop acting – but his words are embedded like footprints all the way along Coronation Road. 'Your mum's turned you against me, hasn't she? I don't suppose you even love your poor old father any more.'

'Of course I do,' Michael says.

And Michael is amazed at how incredibly handsome his father is. Rugged and weather beaten, with actorly eyes that twinkle at whatever audience he is trying to woo, even the audience of his son.

'You aren't a waste of space,' Michael says, his voice a squeak that echoes backwards and forwards over the muddy brown swirl of the Avon. 'Of course you aren't.'

The herring gull is calling out, questioning the existence of fish.

*to the bridge*

Michael sits opposite his father on the edge of his tidy bed. He was always tidy, even as a child – folding his pyjamas beneath the pillows, putting his clothes neatly into his small chest of drawers, keeping his books in alphabetical order on the shelf above the bed. His father sits in the chair that he always sits in, with the polished wooden arms and the backrest carved into a lion's head and mane, the chair he wore smooth reading Winnie the Pooh and The Owl and the Pussycat and Charlie and the Chocolate Factory and The Hobbit and The Twits and the Lord of the Rings. But now he's uncomfortable. Now he uncrosses his legs, leans back into the chair until it creaks with age.

*He's even less comfortable than me,* Michael thinks, *though I'm stuck up here and he's long since moved away.*

And Roger's smile is certainly history. The twinkle in his gaze has evaporated like the morning mist. His eyes are clouding over, maybe even with tears. Michael has finally got through to him, his unconditional love revealing Roger to himself – and it is not a pretty sight. Vanity, selfishness and egotism vie with one another for supremacy. For once in his life, fleetingly self-aware, Roger looks humbled, defeated.

Even now, after all the time that has passed, Michael can't forgive himself.

An earnest stranger sits there, gazing at his son. Pinned against the sky, unsupported, Michael reaches out his arms. He says, in his father's voice because for a moment he has become his father, 'Come here, boyo…' And then, in mock Berkshire, 'Come over 'ere me old mucker and give your disaster area of a dad a grand old hug.'

The naked, weightless Michael tries to hug the man his father was – but his arms just pass through air.

There's nothing there.

Clifton Suspension Bridge wavers behind him. Time and matter flicker in and out of focus – as if it is by no means certain that a universe of matter and energy exists after all.

As if this is all just another of Brunel's jokes.

Even better than the last.


Long ago, when Michael leapt into the abyss, he took a juddering inhalation of the cold, wintry air. He had thought this would be his last chance to breath, his last stab at inhaling more of the planet's wonderful oxygen and nitrogen and carbon dioxide mix

*to the bridge*

than he had ever inhaled before – his last opportunity to breath in everything that could possibly be breathed, to *inhale* Bristol and the surrounding hills, to assimilate inside himself the rising slopes of Leigh Woods, the leisurely sweep of Ashton Court, the lawns beneath Cabot's Tower, the aurora of the sun, the lovely blue sky – his last chance to draw it all in, internalising everything, hauling in, hand over fist, *the world,* and, in the process of internalisation, externalising everything that it was to be Michael Germain.

*He* was what it was.

*He* was the line of trees along Clifton Down Road, curling back towards the Downs.

*He* was the terrace of Georgian houses leading up towards Saville Place.

*He* was the stationary flow of traffic clogging the dual carriageway beside the river.

*He* was Montpelier and Knowle West, St Pauls, St Werburghs, St Andrews.

His fingernails and hair were the Mercs and Vauxhalls, the Fords and Minis, the Morris Minors and Triumphs, and even the horse-drawn cabs and carts populating this haphazard aggregate of time and space.

He was the torrent of light the houses and factories and castles and offices of Bristol had thrown up towards the sky in their thousand year defiance of the night.

He was the iron-knuckled chain tensed against the weight of the bridge.

He was the sewers and the guttering and the gas pipes and the water mains stretching away like nerve and vein beneath the streets of the city.

His ribs were the metal bars reaching down from the sweeping chain to grip the tarmac'd width of Clifton Suspension Bridge.

He –

But it wasn't his last breath after all.

He can still breathe.

His nostrils dilate.

His lungs charge up from the wellspring of life.

That moment hadn't been his last moment, after all.

It hadn't been his last chance.

*This* moment may be his last moment, may be his last chance.

*This* may be his moment of religion.

For Michael Germain has never before felt so far away from death.

He has never before felt so alive.

His lungs are holding him up, powering his chest like twin hot air balloons suspended high above the surface of the Avon.

The water that waits below shows little interest in receiving him – tidal, salty, oozing, limitlessly patient.

The sky of which he has become a part shows little interest in releasing him – the jet trails lazily awaiting the dispersal of the wind.

And someone has written in the firmament:

## Michael…

## Michael Germain…

## …look around you!

## This…

## …is your life.

So yes, he is up here, and he has left behind his wife and home, his ambitions, dreams, his career, his friends, everything he has ever possessed or desired or known, even his clothes… but he's not yet falling.

After all, why should he be?

Where's the hurry?

What's the rush?

## Chapter Eleven

The tower on the south side of the bridge, Leigh Tower, is named after the woodland that rises up the flanks of the south side of the gorge. The abutment beneath the tower, supporting it, is not solid. Records of its construction have been lost, but there are twelve hollow chambers beneath the red sandstone in whose stale air who knows what or who knows who lingers…

The tower at the north end of the bridge is called Clifton Tower.

Neither of the towers are as ornate as the ironic Brunel, in his mid-twenties, designed them to be. Subsequent, more pragmatic, more cost aware engineers cast aside his plans for minarets and sphinxes and produced a far more fitting edifice to their master's genius: an elegant, functional bridge which would have filled even the builders of the pyramids with awe.

The whole bridge moves, but the movement is not transmitted into the towers.

The chain link that supports the roadway rests, in chambers at the top of each tower, on iron saddles which allow the bridge to sway without transmitting that sway into the brick and stone of the tower that supports them. Without those saddles the towers would have cracked and fallen within years of their construction.

The chains pass through the chambers at the tops of the towers, curve over the iron saddles, then stretch down towards ground level and are embedded in ten metre tunnels packed with concrete and brick.

If Michael were to perform a half somersault he would be able to look back beneath the bridge, to witness – his gaze cutting through time and space – the painstaking assembling of the chains, the workmen with their chapped and bleeding hands, the cursing gang leaders more afraid of Brunel's scathing tongue than of the great drop beneath their feet, the winches, the pulleys, the construction basket hanging from a four centimetre diameter steel pole stretched right across the valley.

But Michael isn't about to perform a somersault of any description.

He isn't feeling too agile just now, or even very much in control.

Stasis is losing its grip on him.

Clifton Suspension Bridge is just an eye-catching backdrop.

Michael Germain is beginning to fall.

But perhaps there is some slight chance that he can save himself. If he twists quickly and reaches out behind him – long-armed and long-fingered as he is – perhaps he might still catch the curved end of one of the latitudinal spars that run beneath the roadway, locking his fingers with superhuman strength upon the only substantial human construction near to hand.

Is this his final lifeline, thrown out to him by Brunel's ghost?

Has the obsessive insomniac – sleepless still – at last come good?

No.

The engineer's errant spirit is not the compassionate sort. Brunel was always dismissive of human weakness, or, at least, of all human weakness except his own – and the bridge and its appearance of permanence and strength were only ever a protracted Isambard joke.

It would have been more laughable still if they had left the sphinxes perched at the top of the towers as he had designed them.

What a hoax on the Phoenician-obsessed Victorians!

And – ha ha ha – the spar is already too far away to catch.

*Take your hat off to Nietzsche...* Michael fleetingly thinks.

*Some men are supermen – and some are not.*

## Chapter Twelve

All the same, he cannot help but admire his situation.

He can sense more than see – since vision only touches the surface of things – the tumbledown buildings on the flank of the gorge, the dual carriageway following the river into the heart of Bristol, the sky as taut as a child's belly over the Cumberland Basin, the buildings scattered like wooden blocks from an interrupted child's game.

*How beautiful,* he thinks.

*How elementally, unutterably, indescribably beautiful.*

*And how sad.*

Somewhere on the other side of the docks Michael's mother says, 'You've a poet's eye, Mikey. An eye for the beauty of the world. It's a very special and important talent. It's something your father had too, you know.'

'Doesn't that make it a bad thing, then?'

'Is everything I tell you about your father bad?'

'Almost everything.'

'No, it's not, you silly boy. Don't re-write history. Sometimes I say very nice things about Roger.'

'I'm trying to remember…' Michael mutters.

His mother has just got home. She's bringing in the week's shopping – seven days' worth of food for the one-parent family that she and Michael have become since Roger left. Michael has found a spider under the sink and is carrying it around in a tea cup. She says, 'You are a cruel boy, Mikey, to judge me like that, as if looking down at me from a great height. Perhaps you are more like your father than I'd hoped.'

'Dad doesn't like spiders.'

'He doesn't like a lot of things.'

'People should admire spiders… All they want to do is live and eat and reproduce, just like humans.'

'Is that what you are thinking about now? Reproduction?'

'No! Of course not! You know what I mean.'

'I'm not sure I do – and don't bring that horrible thing any closer, you morbid adolescent!'

'What I don't understand is why Nature would design something like this... Why create something so complicated when something much simpler would do? And why decorate it so beautifully?'

'*Nature* didn't decorate it.' Jane begins putting away the shopping. There's the hint of a smile on her lips, as if she's recognising in Michael the feelings that she has struggled with herself for so very long. 'And *Nature* didn't design it. No one designed it, Mikey. Except maybe God.'

Isn't it a shame that it has taken up until now, almost a metre out from the balustrade of Clifton Suspension Bridge, for him to rediscover his poet's eye? He's still only moving at a snail's pace, but already nearer the surface of the river, a metre closer or maybe two... and it has taken this final assertion of control, of saying, 'My life is my own, to do with as I will!' to remind him of how beautiful the world is, how wonderful it is to be alive – to remind him of the near-intelligent perfection of the thorax of a spider, of the stunning complexity of the sprawl of the city.

And the past and the future are spread out before him too, unveiled in all their confusion like an adolescent snapshot of the perpetual dance of matter and energy and time: Michael's life... and the terraces of Southville, their skylights glinting, their small dense gardens caught in winter's grip; Michael's father in the chair with the carved wooden back... and the three tobacco warehouses clustered between the river and the docks; his father's strong fingers curling over the rounded ends of the chair's arms... and the single track railway to Portishead, overgrown with weeds.

His father's hands are stubby and strong with a potency that Michael will never now achieve. He wonders, *If this is who I come from, if I am born of his flesh, of his genes, why am I so much less masculine than he is, so much less of a man?*

*Why have I never been able to stamp my identity upon the world in the way that he so easily manages to do?*

Roger pushes himself to his feet, reaches forward, ruffles Michael's hair, then turns and leaves the room. Michael listens to his footsteps as he makes his way downstairs and leaves the house. Through the window he watches his father stumble over the paving slabs that lead to the garden gate. Roger is walking away from their

*to the bridge*

family home forever, in favour of a flat in Hackney and a string of affairs with celebrity-hungry starlets. Michael waves after him but Roger doesn't look back.

Roger will never see this particular little boy, in this particular home, ever again.

That is what time does to us.

It steals us from one another, time and time again.

As Roger walks away he is obscured from Michael's view by the uplift of the housing development on the north side of the Bristol docks. They are buildings which have the feeling of the sea about them, of seaside chalets with makeshift balconies and pastel-coloured walls. Rank upon rank, year after year, each block of flats steals the view of its predecessor until the newest are forced to build themselves on pillars thrust deep into the ancient mud. A small tremor, a minor quake, and down they will come, tumbling into the diesel-resplendent water.

Each block emerges from its exoskeleton of scaffolding and planks and perceives itself as *luxury condominium* – until its luxury is superseded by a newer block rising up in front of it with an even better view of the south of Bristol, of the S.S. Great Britain, of the Cumberland Basin, of Ashton Court.

*Life is like that*, Michael thinks as he begins to fall a little faster. *Full of irony and loss.*

This isn't a new thought for him. He once wrote,

> We are constantly searching for permanence, but that's not what life is like, is it?
> Life is just a joke, played on us by a malign god, full of irony and loss.

He once wrote,

> I wish that I could find, somewhere deep within my heart, an end to all these doubts, a place of deep and lasting peace...

Well, perhaps he's found that place. Perhaps he's heading there now.

Even from the foremost of the condominiums the view is paltry compared with the view from the bridge. From the bridge Bristol is framed by the descending flanks of the gorge, the crescents of Clifton Village, the green swathes of Ashton Court. The water in the docks glitters with reflected sunlight and the triad of tobacco warehouses stand guard between the docks and the river, their brick-red rectangular facades holding up mile-high corridors of sky.

In one warehouse Imperial Tobacco still have their offices, where, until recently, the company's employees were energetically encouraged to smoke.

Smoke while you work, was their slogan. An affirmative way to pass the time of day.

The resurrected site guard has lit up already. A long-time functionary, re-birthed at Michael's whim, he watches his fellow employees in and out of the warehouse with a cough that leaves blood speckling the palm of his hand.

'State your business,' he asks.

*'The import and export of tumours?'*

…but tumours don't need cigarettes to summon them into existence.

Roger, Michael's father, smokes like a trooper… and Sarah never smoked.

*Dad's probably lighting up right now,* Michael thinks. *Flicking a burnt-out matchstick into the kitchen sink and gazing from his window onto the back yard of his decaying Hackney tenement.*

*He's smoked for years.*

*He's going to go on smoking.*

*He won't get cancer – or, at least, not until he's very, very old.*

*Not like Sarah.*


*Life just isn't fair.*


With 20:20 vision Michael inspects their little house on Sylvia Avenue – his gaze penetrating the drawn curtains to expose the musky bedroom, the two of them together, on the very evening that he discovered Sarah's tumour.

The moment is imprinted in the spaces of their home like a network of steel girders, like concrete and plaster and long wooden joists, as real and immediate as the nearest of the tobacco warehouses.

Coronation Road, heading east alongside the river, points its multiply-jointed finger spectrally, even joyfully, towards that moment.

*to the bridge*

It is very dark in their bedroom but they are both completely awake. The Avon pours down its long narrow channel towards the Severn Estuary from the space between Sarah's thighs.

*Isn't it strange,* Michael is thinking as he stands beside the bed, *that even after all this time I am still so entranced by your nakedness that it seems to bestow upon me some tremendous sort of honour?*

He thinks things like that, and writes them in his diary, every day.

He is something of an insomniac. Like Brunel, he cannot sleep in the way that other people sleep. He tosses and turns, the muscles of his face as tight as the sinews of a gymnast. He keeps a torch, a pencil, a small black diary beside the bed. When he grows impatient with lying sleepless in the dark he fishes out his diary and muses in writing on the meaning of life.

> What does it all mean?
>
> What the fuck does all of this mean? – And why should it matter what it means, if it means anything at all?

Mildred – Auntie M – will read a few of his observations during her visit to Michael's house. She will mutter 'My goodness!' and shake her head in amusement and disgust. Then, looking up at the sterile good taste of Michael and Sarah's living room, she will murmur, 'Isn't it amazing... I must say I really can't believe it... Isn't it amazing what can happen in a person's head!'

Kneeling before him in a landscape of rooftops and washing lines Sarah gazes into his eyes through the dark.

'There's no need to stand to attention,' she says.

'Oh yes there is,' Michael replies.

He's upright before her at the foot of the bed, erect as a grenadier, grinning like an idiot, smiling down into the lovely eyes of his lovely wife.

She shimmies across the duvet and leans against him, her nipples hard against his ribs. As he explores the perfect articulation of her spine she kisses the line of his collar bone, her hands slipping over his chest then around, down his back and over his buttocks. One of her hands slides forward, circling his hip, taking him in her grip.

*If there is a heaven,* Michael will always remember thinking, *then this is it.*
*What could be more wonderful or more perfect than this?*

*The view from Clifton Suspension Bridge?*
*A satellite image of the planet Earth?*

Geisha-like Sarah bows before him and lowers the crown of her head to rest against his belly.

Moonlight falls through the blinds to lie in bars of gold across her spine.

His first ejaculation is in her mouth – and he's filled to the bursting point with a kind of insane gratitude, a great internal shout of joy.

*What sort of fool,* he wonders, *would ever let this go?*


They enjoy making love when they are both a little drunk. There is no urgency or hurry – and Sarah's orgasms are postponed by the alcohol. More primordial than primeval, his sense of touch and taste and smell take over as he nuzzles her armpits, the long stretch of her thighs, her vulva. With the tips of his fingers and the palms of his hands and even with his belly he marks out the full extent of his territory, stakes ownership to every part of her. He loves the sweep of skin from just beneath her collar bone to her breast, the crease between her buttocks and the back of her thighs, the angularity of her hips. He puts his ear to her chest and listens as intently as a saboteur for the distant hint of tremor, for the involuntary thrust of her hips, as he slips his fingers into her vagina and tries to learn what makes her tick.

Later, tracing the aisle between her breasts, then down, possessively, over her flat stomach and into the mesh of her pubic hair, then around the curve of her waist, he discovers something new.

In that sense, at least, it will always be his.

He is its discoverer… its owner… its proprietor.

Finders, keepers…

Losers, weepers.


Transfixed, gazing out across the Bristol landscape, Michael asks himself if he should have placed a flagpole upon that strange unnatural mound rising slightly to the left and just above the nape of Sarah's spine.

'What is it?' Sarah whispers as he lies there, suddenly still. 'What are you doing?'

Now there was a question worth asking.

One he is asking himself even now.

In his diary he would write,

> It was like discovering an intruder in my wife's body. An invader – but definitely a male invader. It was like discovering someone who in this act of penetration had defiled Sarah and staked his claim upon her. It was like finding someone else's cock beneath my hand, pressing up through Sarah's flesh.

'Haven't you felt it?'

'Felt what?'

'This.'

His penis, perpetually hard inside her as they lie together, abruptly slips free. It is suddenly as devoid of life as the penis of a corpse. He takes her hand and guides it to her back. Her fingers search for a moment – she inhales – lies very still – says nothing. Then she's no longer next to him but standing in front of the mirror with the light on, twisting around, trying to see… and he's on the edge of the bed feeling naked and exposed and more than a little frightened. Even the room feels exposed and naked, as if conscious of an observer watching them through the drawn curtains, as if the very fabric of the house is aware that a persecutor from some distant, terrible height has fixed them in his gaze. Michael fleetingly wishes he had made their home more comfortable, more homely, more a place where children might want to play. He stares at the elegantly bare walls, then back at Sarah. 'We'd better go and find a doctor… Someone who can tell us what it is.'

Sarah turns to look at him. Her eyes are wide and dark and there are tears glinting on her cheeks. She shakes her head, as if amazed at his obdurateness. 'Oh, Michael – no one needs to tell us what it is! It's obvious, isn't it?' Then she's twisting around again, trying to inspect the base of her spine in the mirror. 'It's cancer, Michael. Some weird sort of cancer. There's no use hiding from it. I'm going to die.'

## Chapter Thirteen

His mother lost his father to a rising star – but in the end found God. The process took a hundred detours and countless years but like a slowly growing tumour it eventually consumed her. The longest interlude of sanity was during her affair with Geraint, a Welsh academic with invasive halitosis whom Michael and Mildred never grew to like. Under the anaesthesia of his breath Jane forgot the holy trinity and the fatal attraction of the sublime. She turned her back on Jesus and all that *He* had to offer. People can do that: black-hole all awareness of the cancer inside them. But she returned to God full time when the lecturer returned to his wife. It was both a parting of ways and a parting of the waves. Around that time Michael, too, left home, taking up a job in London.

His mother's parents had been Catholic. Much to everyone's disgust she capitulated in her middle age to her childhood superstitions. It was something Michael had never been able to understand. What did God have to do with anything? What had God ever done for him?

Nothing.

Not, at least, until now.

But now, half a dozen metres from the balustrade of Clifton Suspension Bridge, he begins to suspect that there is, after all, a higher meaning beneath the inchoate substance of the material world. Flying in the face of his materialism is the sheer beauty of the mess of tarmac and cars, of washing lines and red tiled roofs, of 1925 intermingling with 2012 and 1899, of people sauntering down the pathways of their lives towards Prince Street Bridge and the city centre…

He thinks, *Might there be something in* God, *after all? Is it possible that He, or some other, alien intelligence, despite all my scepticism and doubt, has had a hand in constructing this?*

And yet Clifton Suspension Bridge, strung out behind him across the gorge, is just a bridge.

The lives of the men who are building the bridge, scaling the heights even now, and the lives of their wives, are just lives.

The children in the launch day crowd, clapping and squealing as Brunel finishes his speech, are just children – soon to grow up, grow old and die.

What, Michael wonders, can be more irreligious, more sad or more mundane than a child growing up?

An adult falling down?

And Michael is definitely falling now.

For a few fractions of a second he fell relatively slowly.

Some kind of inner reluctance – an inertia born of fear – held him back.

But now an irresistible force has him in its grip, is holding him by his ankles, is hauling him down towards the river. It is the weight of the earth that has caught him. The earth's massive bulk is drawing him in.

Michael is falling at last and the speed of his fall is rapidly increasing, accelerating towards a terminal velocity.

He is falling ten metres per second faster each second.

That is the acceleration of an object near the surface of the earth.

The acceleration of gravity.


In the supermarket car park, bigger than the sprawling buildings of the shop itself, is Sarah's hospital bed. They have cut out the tumour and she is lying there unconscious, her lovely face undreaming, her eyes closed. Michael sits beside her with his face in his hands.

He was at her side, watching her slip into unconsciousness, as they counted backward from ten. Then, while they operated, he waited in the corridor outside the operating theatre for almost three hours. He rehearsed, as he waited, his reactions to Sarah dying under anaesthesia. He rehearsed the surgeon wandering out, grim faced, and offering a dozen variations on, 'I'm afraid it's not good news, Mr Germain… I'm very, very sorry'.

Sometimes, in his rehearsals, Michael saw himself going berserk, killing the surgeon and the anaesthetist, nurses, a patient in a wheelchair. Scalpels peppered the waiting rooms and the corridors like a medical remake of The House of Flying Daggers.

Or sometimes he simply staggered beneath the impact of the words, then remained leaning against the wall woodenly nodding – and going on nodding until they dosed him with pentathol and led him away to the hospital's secure psychiatric ward.

Sometimes in his rehearsals of untimely bereavement he wept – and the tears flooded from his eyes in a tidal wave that tore the hospital loose of its foundations and washed it down into the Avon gorge. He would be there amongst the bodies and the debris, bobbing along in a self-made ocean of self-pity and grief.

Now he really is weeping – but not because Sarah has died but because she is still alive.

Because he can't believe his luck.

A couple of days before Sarah's operation, in the space somewhere beyond Brandon Tower and St Michael's Hill, Dr Falatino summons Sarah and Michael into a cubicle in Oncology Day Beds. The room is very bare and utilitarian, the way Michael once liked rooms to be. There are two moulded plastic chairs, a desk and a stool, little else. Waving them to the chairs, Dr Falatino says, 'I'll be very frank with you, Sarah... Michael. I'll be frank because that is always the best option in the long run, to know the facts of the situation, at least as best we can.'

'We like frankness,' Michael says.

'Then, to be as frank as possible, if this is the type of cancer that we have every reason to believe it is, then I'm afraid we are faced with a cancer that is very aggressive indeed.'

'Terminal?' Michael asks, trying to out-blunt the consultant. 'Is that what you mean? Is Sarah going to die?'

'Renal carcinomas can be terminal,' Dr Falatino says.

'How often is "can be"?'

Michael is speaking for both of them, asking Sarah's questions as well as his own. In situations like this he often takes the lead, sometimes with a sense of embarrassment, a secret acknowledgement that it is the wrong thing to do. Sarah is not a child. She is an adult, with a home, a husband, a successful career. But today he feels no shame. Today his fully conscious intention is to act as a buffer between his beautiful wife and the frightening new reality into which the two of them have somehow stumbled. He wants to be Sarah's interpreter and bodyguard, both. He says, 'How many people die of this sort of cancer, and since when?'

Dr Falatino: 'Since... when?'

'Yes,' Michael insists. 'What proportion? What percentage? What is the survival rate? Surely there are statistics? Aren't there case studies? Surely you can give us something a little more scientific than "can be terminal"?'

His voice sounds loud in his ears – too loud.

'It's not quite that simple,' the consultant says. 'It very much depends on the type of renal carcinoma it turns out to be. In general, in adults, renal cancer is very rare.'

'We don't need simple, Dr Falatino. Sarah can cope with complex – and even I can sometimes. We just want the hard-nosed facts – so that we know what we've got to deal with, what we've got to face.'

Dr Falatino is a fat woman in a white smock. Glasses perch on her small nose; her chest heaves each time she inhales to speak. She looks from Michael to Sarah speculatively, as if trying to understand their relationship, as if assessing what she can and cannot say. Michael fights the impulse to go down on his knees before her and beg for Sarah's life, contradicting the tough-minded attitude he is trying to display. It is an impulse he will need to resist every hour upon the hour or even more often than that in the following months. Everything rests on Dr Falatino and her colleagues. Everything rests on the nurses and the doctors getting it right. The consultant says, 'What you have to face depends upon the condition of the tumour. If it is stage one, and hasn't broken through its sheath, then patients often survive.'

'That's still too vague, dotctor. How often is "often"? What percentage? Can't you be more specific?' Michael knows he's being insistent, perhaps even rude, but he doesn't care. He doesn't want to hide behind platitudes, half-truths, hints. He wants what he knows Sarah wants: to get to the heart of the matter, to get to the point.

'Michael's right,' Sarah says. 'I do want to know.'

'Statistically, then, well, seventy or eighty per cent of stage one presentations of most renal carcinomas are not fatal.'

Michael asks, 'Is that seventy-five per cent? Or is it nearer seventy-two, or nearer seventy-eight? Can't you be more precise?'

'I'm afraid not, Mr Germain. This is a very rare condition in adults. I'm being too definite as it is. The statistical sample isn't really large enough to be meaningful.'

'And if it's not stage one?'

'I'm afraid that is something you will need to prepare yourselves for. If it is, for example, a rhabdoid tumour, then these are not normally identified before they are at least stage two – because of where they're placed, and because of how long it takes most people to realise that there is anything wrong.'

'Until they've grown so big they get noticed,' Sarah says.

'Yes. Precisely.'

Michael: 'So if it's a stage two…'

'Do you really want to talk about this in such black and white terms?' The consultant turns her gaze on Sarah. Sarah hasn't put on any make-up or lipstick and her face is anaemic in the consulting room's soft yellow light. Her hands lie as passive as the victims of a murder upon her lap. In the unknown landscape before her lurk the spectres of mutilation and death. It is a landscape entirely different from Michael's. Michael has time at his disposal. He is king of all time.

Sarah nods and Michael says, 'Yes, we'd like to know. We need to know.' He reaches out and takes Sarah's hand. 'How else can we prepare ourselves for what's to come?'

'Then I would say that approximately ninety per cent of stage two renal carcinomas of this type in adults, or in children over the age of ten, prove to be fatal. If this is the tumour we expect it to be, then it is a highly aggressive and very dangerous condition.'

'Is there – is there any hope that it is not what you think it is? That it's – what's the word for it? – benign?'

'In this location… in a kidney… and this fast growing… it is very unlikely that our diagnosis, even if provisional, is wrong.'

'When will you know for sure? Isn't there something you can do straight away? A biopsy or something like that?'

'We would normally consider a biopsy… but with aggressive cancers there is a degree of risk.'

'Just sticking in a needle – ?'

'…can breach the capsule enclosing the tumour. If there's any hope that it is still a stage one tumour there's a small risk that a biopsy might take it to stage two. No, I'm afraid we really need to act quickly. We need to remove the entire right kidney and perhaps some of the surrounding tissue as a matter of urgency.'

Michael starts to speak but Sarah interrupts him. 'And then leave me with a ten per cent or less chance of survival? Why would I want that? I'd rather just go home…'

'But we don't know yet. Your chances may be a seventy-five per cent or greater... There is a chance – and this is what we need to be sure of – that your condition is still stage one.' Dr Falatino adjusts the glasses perched on the bridge of her nose. 'It is important that we operate, just to make sure of our facts – and facts, I think we agreed, are what we all want...'

Sarah shrugs. 'If you put it that way... Yes. Operate... Let's just get it over and done with.'

Dr Falatino smiles. She clearly likes Sarah. Her glance towards Michael is a little less warm. Overprotective husbands are always a trial. 'I'll put things in motion,' she says. 'The hospital will ring you up this afternoon – and I very much hope we are talking about an operation in the next twenty-four to thirty-six hours.'


The surgeon, Mr Reece, and the consultant, Dr Falatino, walk down the corridor towards Michael in close conversation. Both are animated, even cheerful, as if they've just solved a crossword which has been puzzling them for days. Michael assumes he may not need to go berserk and kill the entire population of the hospital including himself. The surgeon takes his arm. 'Good news, I believe,' he says. He is as thin as a rake, narrow shouldered and narrow hipped, with an intense, narrow face. If Dr Falatino hugged the surgeon he would vanish into her ample bosom.

'How good?' Michael asks. 'Is it a stage one? Was the sheath still intact?' He hears himself speaking pidgin-medicine: eager savage to the doctor's great white hunter.

'We think so,' Mr Reece says. 'And we believe, I'm pleased to say, that we have removed it all. But let's not get ahead of ourselves. We'll do a scan in a couple of days and speak again then.'


Michael forces a little strength into his spine, straightens up, lowers his hands from his face. Sarah's breath is speeding up. She is drifting towards consciousness. 'It's okay, darling,' he whispers. 'You don't have to worry. Everything's okay.' She opens her eyes, mumbles something too quietly for Michael to catch, then says it again louder: 'He only got to six.'

'Six what, darling?'

'Counting backwards. He only got to six.'

'Oh yes. Yes, you're right. You went out like a light.'

'I feel like laughing, Mikey. Is everything alright? I didn't know what to expect. I feel like laughing with relief. That I'm still alive.'

'Laugh then, sweetheart. Everything's fine. Laugh as much as you want – so long as it doesn't hurt you…'

'I think it's the anaesthetic.' She pulls his hand to her cheek, holds it there. 'Find out for me, darling, where you buy this stuff?'

He's having to work hard at it, but he's managing not to cry.

'They think they've got it all out,' he says. 'They think it's a stage one. We'll have you out of here in no time.'

'That's wonderful,' she murmurs, beginning to fall asleep again.

'Yes, wonderful,' Michael whispers.

But five days later she's back in that very same hospital bed, and the poisoning with vincristine, ifosfamide, actinomycin and epirubicin has begun.

## Chapter Fourteen

The river is waiting for him, as hard as iron plate.

His eyes are bare slits and the world is flying past.

How should he hit the water? Feet first, bracing his knees for impact?

Would that be the best way to survive?

Isambard is falling too. Michael can see him out of the corner of his eye. The engineer's cigar sizzles like a firework. His eyebrows dance with an electricity all of their own. His eyes are sparkling with intelligence and a grim, electric wit.

What happens, Michael wonders, when ghosts experience a fatal impact?

Do they die, too?

Sarah says, 'I feel dizzy, Mikey, and my wee is the colour of blood.'

'That's the epirubicin,' Michael says.

'And you look ill. Are you sure you're getting enough sleep?'

'I don't need to sleep.'

'Everyone needs to sleep.'

'I've forgotten how.'

'You must look after yourself, Michael. You need to sleep and eat properly. This illness of mine shouldn't take over everything. You need to keep on living your life. For both of us.'

'This is my life, sweetheart. Right here at your side.'

'It shouldn't be,' Sarah says. 'We need it not to be. I need to know that you're alright. That you'll cope. That you'll be okay... if I die.'

No.

Landing feet first will simply drive his tibia up through his knee caps, his femur up through his pelvis, his pelvis into his abdomen, his compacted cervical vertebrae like the bolt of a humane killer up into his brain.

It might be the impact with the water that does that, or it might be the impact with the mud beneath the water.

Face down, then? Flat on?

*to the bridge*

Isambard is watching him, still upright and unperturbed as he falls, his long sideburns framing a face of unexpected kindness and wisdom. "Go for it, son," he murmurs. "You'll be alright."

At least then, face down, flat on, he would see what was coming: the wall of dirty brown water rising towards him at motorway speed, the outline of a pike just beneath the surface, his own shadowy reflection coalescing and becoming concrete.

No.

That's not the way to do it.

So he's there at her side for every single moment of her first cycle of chemotherapy, guarding her against the dangers of this strange new world. He watches as they tape something called a cannula to her wrist, a needle permanently inserted into a vein, allowing the drip-feed of medicine. She shows him the scar where they have removed the whole of her left kidney, fourteen centimetres long and already beginning to heal – and he almost faints.

A handsome young doctor tries to explain. 'Cells are more sensitive to being killed when they are replicating,' he says, 'and cancer cells in general replicate quickly. Chemotherapy takes advantage of that fact – uses that window of opportunity to get at the cancer. Unfortunately, hair follicles and bone marrow cells also replicate quickly, which is why your hair falls out and your white blood cell level goes down and we have to protect you from infection.'

'I see.' This is Michael – though he is too tired to see very much at all.

'You do?'

'Thank you for explaining it to us,' Sarah says.

The doctor retreats, a little perplexed by their apparent lack of interest. Michael mutters. 'I probably know more about the drugs they are giving you than he does… Oh, the joys of the internet.'

'The joys of being poisoned,' Sarah says.

'Yes, that too.'

But it's not just Sarah who is filling up with poison.

Michael is also becoming toxic. A poisonous velocity is pumping through his veins, driving him forward, downward, at an ever greater speed; driving him at breakneck speed to and from the hospital each day, carelessly swerving around cyclists, tyre-treading the toes of pedestrians, tail-gating geriatrics in their geriatric cars, undertaking buses, overtaking trucks, rushing helter-skelter from one uncomfortable space to another.

He is accelerating, faster and faster all the time. He is going faster and Sarah is slowing down, both of them growing more and more toxic with every passing second. There is a bitterness at the back of his throat, burning like acid, burning like regret. He hadn't thought through his options, had he? He hadn't taken the time to work this all out before he jumped.

So should he try, he wonders, to fall head first – spearing down towards the muddy water in an Olympic-style dive?

His hands and wrists will shatter on impact.

Either with the water or with the mud.

His forearms and the bones in his upper arms will concertina like folded paper.

The vertebrae of his neck will punch a channel down into his chest.

His lungs will compress to the size of two clenched fists.

This is not a game.

The calculus of survival is not a science. It is not even an art.

That's a secret the unfathomable Isambard knows only too well. Michael can see that from his smile.

No, the best way to hit the water will be to turn through the air so that he falls on his back, looking up towards the sky.

He has always loved the sky – as blue as Sarah's eyes, as deep and unforgiving as the depths of Sarah's soul.

But why is he worrying about the best way to fall?

Would anything he does make a difference?

At a time like this, can there be a *best* way?

Very quickly the cycles of Sarah's incarceration became apparent. Three or four days in Ward 31 for chemotherapy, followed by a few days at home when they both feel like refugees from a distant war. Their needs during Sarah's brief vacations from medication are very different. They try to talk but he wants to talk about her illness, about the medicines they are giving her, about the research he's done on the internet into the repercussions of taking vincristine and ifosfamide and actinomycin, about which nurse is incompetent and which nurse is kind, about which doctor strikingly intelligent and which in a hurry to work down the conveyor belt of faceless and uninvolving patients – about anything and everything to do with her survival – but Sarah doesn't want to think about that at all. Sarah wants to phone up friends from work and talk for hours about the state of her business, or, when not doing that, to talk to Michael for hours about the state of his telecommunications company, about why he should be doing more in the way of networking while she's away in hospital, not less. She wants to talk about the state of the world, about inflation, about house prices, about the loose step below the front door, about the garden, while he wants to analyse her illness from the inside out, to take it by the throat and shake it until it squeaks. When friends come to dinner Sarah embraces them, kisses them, holds their hands, while Michael phones them in advance and tells them to disinfect themselves, not to come if they have even the slightest symptom of a cold, not even to breath on Sarah if they can possibly help it…

He writes in his diary, trying to make a joke of his obsession,

> Neutropenia, neutropenia,
> So much worse than a seizure
> It's the one and only geeza
> Neutropenia, neutropenia

Neutropenia is when the chemotherapy slows down the bone marrow's production of white blood cells, when they can no longer protect you and any infection, even the common cold, can kill.

Then Sarah gets ill just as he expected – predicted – warned that she would.

*Bloody friends! Bloody bone marrow! Bloody everything!*

And they pack Sarah's things for hospital and rush from their peaceful home back to the noise and hubbub of Ward 31. Solicitous nurses connect Sarah to her intravenous drip while she drifts in and out of consciousness, tossing and turning, wired up for saline, IV antibiotics, anti-nausea drugs, god knows what, her temperature checked hourly, her blood pressure checked every three or four hours, and Michael spending whole nights at her bedside chewing on his knuckles.

Then she gets better. She always gets better. They return home for a few days. Then it's back to Ward 31 for the next cycle of chemotherapy.

Michael loathes even the names of the drugs.

Vincristine: derived from the evergreen flowering shrub Vinca Rosea, causing numbness, tremors, nausea, malaise, interfering with the growth of rapidly developing cells.

Ifosfamide, a clear colourless fluid with the potential to damage the kidney and bladder.

'What's that?' he asks as the nurse temporarily disconnects the drip and injects something new.

'Mesna,' the nurse says. 'To stop the bladder bleeding. Counters the affects of the Ifos.'

Ifosfamide: causes nausea and vomiting and dizziness. Affects fertility. Interferes with the DNA of blood cells and decreases white blood cell count. Causes neutropenia ten to fourteen days after treatment.

Then there's actinomycin. Taking two or three minutes to deliver via a syringe, derived from bacteria that live in soil. Causes hair loss, mouth ulcers, anorexia. In the grip of this drug Sarah is growing thinner than Michael has ever known her. It interferes with the genetic material of cells, causing a low platelet and white blood cell count. Because of this, it won't be a good thing if bleeding starts.

Epirubicin. Red. Turns your urine the colour of blood. Sometimes causes cardiac damage and infertility.

Cisplatin. Makes your fingers tingle.

Etoposide. Carboplatin.

All of them toxic. Some of them carcinogenic. Some of them increase your risk of cancer much, much later, when you think you are better, when you think you are safe. All of them cancer suppressing and sometimes even cancer curing.

Who would have thought that this poisoner's pharmacopoeia could possibly prove so useful?

Who would have thought that the human body could survive such abuse?

The hospital bed, the nurses, the doctors, the hospital itself – all these things have become an integral part of Michael and Sarah's lives. 'We are becoming *old hands*,' Sarah says. 'It's funny to see the new people arriving. Not *funny* funny... funny sad... how confused and lost and dazed they seem. Sometimes I feel like getting out of bed and going and telling them not to be so afraid, that this is just an everyday occurrence, that this hospital is a normal place that normal people come to, to try and deal with illnesses that are in fact completely commonplace. Illness and death are commonplace, really, aren't they? I don't want to go on pretending that they are a complete surprise anymore – as if they're something that most of us will never have to deal with at some point in our lives.'

'None of this seems very normal to me,' Michael says.

'But it is,' Sarah insists. 'What's not normal is how the whole world out there cocoons itself from reality. And what's also not normal is how little sleep you're letting yourself get. Just look at you. You'll start to hallucinate before very long.'

*Before very long?*

Michael is hallucinating already.

Sometimes he imagines he can see the universe flung out before him like a chess board, mono-dimensional: time, space, everything compressed – that he is just floating above it, a witness to events that really have nothing to do with him, a detached observer without any connection to the here and now.

Sarah says, 'You mustn't let yourself become a victim of this illness of mine.'

'And let you be a victim all alone?'

'I'm not a victim, Michael. I won't let that happen. Even if I die I won't be a victim.' She pushes herself upright in her bed. 'I'm not going to be pathologised by this.'

'No, I can see that...' and he thinks, *She's stronger than me. She's here in Ward 31, operated on, poisoned by vile chemotherapeutical drugs, and she's stronger than me. It's weird. It's wonderful but it's weird.* And he lies, 'And I won't let myself be, either.'

In the bed opposite an old woman mumbles to herself. Michael makes out the words, 'Please, Miss, I need – I need to go... Please, Miss. Miss? Can I go now, Miss? I need to go...'

'Should I call the nurse?' he whispers.

'No,' Sarah answers. 'She says that all the time. She's got an incontinence bag anyway.'

'And where's yesterday's girl?' Michael asks.

The day before a young woman had been sleeping in the old woman's bed – with an oxygen tube clipped under her nose and her face as white as paper.

'She died in the night.'

'Oh god...'

'It's normal,' Sarah says. 'People die. These things happen. It's just normal.'

Michael looks at her, wondering.

*Normal? A young woman wiped out by cancer like a number deleted from a mobile phone? Like a dress rehearsal for the Germain family: a taste of things to come?*

*Normal?*

*Can that really be normal?*


A nearby window peers out onto the grey concrete wall of another part of the hospital. An equally impersonal window returns its gaze.

Michael likes to stand there, staring out through the glass without seeing anything, an inner landscape stretching away into the distance before him. He imagines he can see, through the concrete and brick, the city centre and the Cumberland Basin, the Lloyds building and @Bristol, the square with the fountains and the sculptures of people just standing around, the strange glass vestibules in the square like waiting rooms for people with nowhere to go: entrances to an underground car park.

Standing before the window he feels as if he has the whole of Bristol mapped out inside him.

He *is* Bristol, he sometimes thinks: inside and out.

Sarah climbs from her bed and pulls her fluids stand over to his side. 'You look as if you've just seen a ghost,' she says. 'Don't look so frightened.'

'I've never been frightened in my life.'

'You're frightened by the thought of me dying. You're afraid you won't cope. You're afraid you won't know what to feel or how to react... I know you are. I'm afraid of all those things too.'

'I'm much more than afraid,' Michael says. His whole body is shaking with fear. 'I'm terrified.'

'But there's something that terrifies me more,' Sarah says.

'The hospital food?'

'No, something that frightens me even more than that.'

'What could be more frightening than hospital food?' He's trying to be funny but not succeeding. His voice is as plaintive as the call of a gull, very far away.

'*You* are, Michael. I'm afraid for *you*. I'm afraid of your not coping. I'm afraid of your not surviving this… this episode in our lives.'

'You don't need to be worried about anything like that. Not on my behalf.'

'Then you'll have to promise me something.'

'I'll try.'

'You'll have to promise me that you will carry on, no matter what. That you will keep living a normal life. That you will work and listen to music and go out with friends and all that sort of thing, no matter what. That you will try to be happy, no matter what happens…'

He looks out across the inhospitable space to the other window. Something flickers past.

*Bird shit.*

'I…'

'You want to help me. I know you do. Well, that's how you can help me. By promising that.'

'I –'

'Don't say anything now. You don't always have to have the answers.'

He turns to her. Pulls her to him. Feels her breath upon his neck. 'You don't have to worry about me,' he whispers. 'I'll be alright.'


When he gets home he wanders through their house like a ghost, not bothering to turn on the lights or even the radio. Then his heart skips a beat and the night is gone. He brushes his teeth, puts on clean clothes, drives through Bristol like a madman, risks other people's lives, risks his own, doesn't care. Arrives at Sarah's bedside with a mug of coffee and a hot baguette, carefree and smiling.

'If you're trying to make yourself ill, it's working,' Sarah says. Her skin is so pale she would be almost invisible against the white cliffs of Dover. 'You look sicker than me. Did you see the way the nurse was looking at you? She was trying to decide which one of us was most in need of treatment. And when did you last shave? Do you really want to grow a beard? You know a beard wouldn't suit you. Do you remember the last time? You looked like Robinson Crusoe's ugly uncle.'

'I'm fine. Really, I am.'

'You're not. Anyone can see.'

'I am. I really am.'

'In your dreams, you are.'

*I don't dream anymore,* Michael wants to say, *at least not when I'm sleeping –* but he bites his tongue. It's true that he's feeling unwell. Sometimes he feels too nauseous to eat, though at other times he gorges himself on whatever comes to hand. One morning he ate a whole loaf of bread and the contents of a jar of peanut butter without noticing what he was doing, then sat there all alone, gearing himself up for his next hospital visit, feeling like he hadn't eaten anything at all and staring into the empty jar.

He eats enough and he doesn't need to sleep. It's difficult to sleep when you're suffering from vertigo. He washes. He brushes his teeth. He's okay. Really he is.

But he writes in his diary,

> *I want to be ill.*
> *I want to be as ill as you, Sarah.*
> *I want to be iller.*
> *I don't want to be left behind.*

## Chapter Fifteen

Dismal Bristol rain, covering everything, immersing the entire city.

Michael is in a traffic jam, in his car. The windscreen wipers sweep backwards and forwards over the glass like the foreplay of a CIA rendition. *Take this… And this… And this…*

In Number 59 Sylvia Avenue the telephone rings.

'Hello?'

*And this.*


In Number 59 Sylvia Avenue the telephone rings.

Without even glancing at Sarah, taking ownership of her son's home since he's vanished off somewhere, god knows where, Jane picks up the phone. 'Hello?'

'This is Isambard.'

'Who?'

'Isambard.'

'Are you a friend of Michael's? Do you know where he is?'

'Where who is?'

'This is Jane, Michael's mother. Do you know where Michael is?'

'Sorry… I may have the wrong number. Or perhaps this instrument is at fault. You understand, telephones with wires were a very clever invention, but these wireless things – of what use are they? Much better to look a man in the eye when you give him the news.'

'Do you have news? News of Michael?'

'I was trying for the Samaritans. Are you they?'

'I'm sorry?'

'Are you they?'

'No. No, I'm afraid – '

Then the prankster disconnects.

'Who was it?' Mildred asks.

'How should I know? A wrong number, I think.'

*to the bridge*

Jane lowers the phone to her lap. She avoids Mildred's inquisitive gaze. A wrong number? Really? Or some sort of a message? That strange conversation had an oracular resonance, as fateful as a missive from the other side.

For once in her life Jane feels unnerved.

Michael. Please come home.

This is your mother.

This is your mother calling.


He squeezes his eyes tightly shut, holding the steering wheel in a white-knuckled grip. His eyelids feel grainy. Another night with no sleep and his car is filling up with exhaust fumes from the cars in front. He turns off the blower and the windscreen immediately begins to mist. Rain hammers on the roof of the car like the pellets of a shotgun, expelled at close range.

Miserable Bristol rain, taking over the world.

He is on his way to the hospital. Of course he is. That is where he is always on his way to these days. The windscreen wipers only just manage to clear the windscreen but he can't see through the glass because of the condensation. Those are his options. Condensation or fumigation. Drive blind or accept the prospect of being gassed alive. He reaches out for the controls. Turns the blower on high, takes a blast of fume-laden air, quickly turns it off again.

'Shit.'

He's feeling like shit.

Sarah, waiting for him in hospital, is as ill as she has ever been. She's feverish, barely able to speak. He was worried she would die while he went home to shower and get clean clothes. He's worried she'll be dead when he gets back.

He's been practicing those funeral speeches again.

He's getting them down pat.

*Don't leave without me.*

*Don't leave without me.*

And the windscreen wipers keep wiping but he can't see a thing.


Yes, he's half-way down now and his vision is impaired.

The world seems darker and more closed in. No more sprawling Bristol landscapes. No more lording it over time and space.

Maybe it's because there are more shadows down here.

It's closer to the river bed, closer to the dark side of the earth.

'Isambard?" he asks, or tries to ask, but the word won't leave his mouth. *Isambard?*

The air is making a whistling sound. He's not sure he can breath.

'Uh – '

He tries to fill his lungs, to complete a single word.

No.

He can no longer breath.


Sarah says, 'You've got to stop doing this.'

She seems a little better, though she's only half-way through her chemotherapy and there's plenty more neutropenia to come. She's shaved off what was left of her hair and even her eyebrows have wasted away to nothing – but the fever, at least for the moment, has gone. It's been replaced by an accusation.

'I'm sorry,' Michael replies, 'for whatever it is that you want me to be sorry for.'

'I'm not sure you really are. I'm almost beginning to think you're enjoying this whole thing – that the poet in you is revelling in the drama of it all.'

'That's a cruel thing to say.'

'Then *I'm* sorry. It's just that sometimes it feels that way... as if even this illness isn't really mine. As if you've taken ownership of it. As if you've taken it over.'

An orderly arrives with food. 'The veggie alternative?' she asks in a strong Polish accent.

'Since when have you been a vegetarian?' Michael asks.

Sarah relaxes. 'I want to be confident I'm not eating ex-patients,' she whispers – and they both begin to laugh.


He wonders in the whistling rush of air if he should roll himself into a ball and hit the surface of the river like an aborted foetus hitting the waste disposal sluice.

*to the bridge*

He wonders if he should hold out his arms to either side and fall towards the water like Jesus Christ outstretched upon the cross.

He wonders if any of this matters.

It's not as if he ever decided he wanted to survive.

## Chapter Sixteen

Before their velocity became too great, Isambard had spat out the butt of his cigar and engaged him in conversation.

Brunel (musing): Have you ever wondered whether this might be little more than self-indulgent bed-wetting? You know, I'm trying to work out why I like you: throwing your life away on a whim!

Michael: Not exactly a whim...

Brunel: Then what is it? A carefully considered action, the result of detailed and extensive planning, executed after much premeditation? I'm not seeing the evidence... It's not as if you built a bridge to get here, submitted draft after draft before it was accepted, assessed minimum weight against maximum strength, measured and calculated and checked and re-checked...

Michael: Not everything needs to be planned in advance. Have you never acted on impulse?

Brunel (clutching his hat to his head as if it might act as some sort of brake): No, never. Or very rarely. It's a dangerous option which often leaves one hanging – out on a limb, one might say.

Michael: Very apposite.

Brunel: My preference is for preparation and precision, as you can see if you look over your shoulder.

Michael: I blame the bridge. Your bridge.

Brunel: *You blame the bridge?*

Michael: Why not? It drew me up here like a magnet, it hauled me onto the balustrade as if I had manacles on my wrists, then it catapulted me out into the open air... You know, none of this would ever have happened if you hadn't entered that competition in the first place... the one to design the bridge. That one that you didn't even win...

Brunel: Can you believe that? I actually had to go in and tell the judges why they were wrong!

Michael: You helped them see sense.

*to the bridge*

Brunel:  So the jumper blames the bridge... In my day –

Michael: Yes?

Brunel:  In my day I would have sacked you for saying a thing like that.

Michael: So sack me.

Brunel (eyeing the river below): It's a little late for that.

Michael: It's never too late. You're the genius. Think of a way to get us out of this.

Brunel:  A plan?

Michael: That might help.

Brunel:  I thought you didn't like plans. Wasn't it spontaneity you were after? A eureka moment? A revelation?

Michael: A plan would be good.

Brunel:  Then tell me, what are those flying machines you all travel around in these days? There's one over there.

Michael: Planes?

Brunel:  Yes. That's what you need. A plane, not a plan. Put out your arms. Learn to fly!

Michael: A useful suggestion. Thank you, Isambard. I guess I'll just have to try.

He leans over and kisses Sarah on the cheek. 'How are you? How are you feeling?'

It's been four whole hours since he crept away, drove home, showered, slept for what felt like ten minutes, grabbed a slice of toast, jumped in the car without brushing his teeth or shaving, drove back to be at her side.

'Come up with another question – I'm tired of that one.'

'Well, aren't you feeling just a little bit better?'

'My fingers tingle all the time. My head hurts. I constantly feel sick. I feel too weak to get up but too uncomfortable to lie still. And I'm still upset about my hair.'

'You're the most beautiful person without hair that I've ever seen.'

'Well, that's not saying much, is it? No, don't ask about me. Talk to me about what you've been doing. I'm sick of thinking about me, Mikey.'

'Then don't. I think about you enough for the both of us.'

'That's not what I want either. You can't live this illness for me…'

He's staring at a puncture wound that the doctors have cut into the space between her shoulder and her neck. *I'm going to try to live this illness for you,* he thinks, *if it's the last thing I do…*

Running out of usable veins for a cannula the doctors have put what they call a *long-line* down through the hollow where her collar bone meets her neck – pushing it four fifths of the way along a major artery towards her heart. It's a convenient way to dispense medicine – though it has its own dangers.

Michael reaches out, touches her shoulder. 'Does it hurt?'

'It will if you touch it.'

He draws back. 'I've brought you something.' He takes the present he's brought her from his pocket, puts it in her palm.

'An iPod?'

'An iPod Touch.'

'What a beauty.' Credit card slim, all screen and no machine.

'I've put all your favourite music on it.'

'You are a sweetheart. I'll listen tonight, when I'm going to sleep.'

'Better than listening to the farting and snoring of the other patients.'

'Or the groaning.' She nods towards a curtained-off bed where a woman has just had her legs removed.

Michael takes her hand, kisses it. 'Do you think the nurses would mind if I stayed tonight? I could bring in a takeaway.'

'I'm sure they wouldn't mind, but I don't think you should. You need more sleep than you're getting and I've got hardly any appetite.'

'You need to eat more than I need to sleep.'

'I know. But not today. Not tonight.'

Later she whispers, 'Let's talk.'

'Okay.' Michael puts down his newspaper. 'I was speaking to Dr Fala – '

'No. Not about my illness. About other things.'

'Um, well… the house is fine. I've fixed the step.'

'And business?'

'Business goes on.'

'You promised you wouldn't let things fall apart…'

'I haven't let anything fall apart. In fact, the FelCo contract has come in.'

'Oh fantastic!'

'Two point five million.'

'You clever boy!'

*to the bridge*

But Michael doesn't feel clever at all. He feels like he's lost his grip on making money, on being a high-flyer, on commerce. What does any of that matter when someone you love is desperately ill? What sort of fragment of a damn does he give for any of the things that he's immersed himself in for so many years? Nothing matters anymore except Sarah staying alive – and spending time beside her, taking ownership of her illness, taking some of the weight off her shoulders. Why should she be alone with this – and why should he? Tears struggle at the back of his eyes at the thought of being alone. Of being here when she's gone. He shows a bit of gumption. He holds his tears in check.

If Michael were able to swivel in the air and look back beneath the underside of the bridge, he would see the shadow of Brunel's lovely creation thrown across the flank of Leigh Woods. Beneath the cover of the trees and the shadows of the towers voles, shrews and other small creatures creep about their business, tiny mammalian children scurrying close upon their heels. Birds hop along the naked boughs, trilling declarations of territorial rights or declarations of love. A dog snuffles amongst the leaves and, too far away to be its owner, a walker with heavy sideburns strolls down one of the gravel paths humming *Years of Pilgrimage* by Franz Liszt.

Why fall? Michael asks himself, sensing all of this. Why keep on falling? Why not just stop.

Why not – he wonders – let his body fall but let his mind stop, suspended where it is, perceiving all that there is to perceive, reaching out to touch with tendrils of thought the rock, the air, the herring gull, the hand of the walker, the dog, the riverbank, the Bristol Whitebeam trees, the Wilmott trees?

Whitebeam trees grow nowhere else in the world but here, in Clifton Gorge.

He, and they, have no other place.

Later he visits the hospital shop, buys a chocolate bar, a magazine, crisps. The girl at the counter seems innocently simple. She takes a thousand years to work out the price of his three purchases, to key them in, to read the display telling her how much change to give him back. Her lips look botoxed, her eyes are as blank as satellite dishes. She allows no opening for communication with her customers, as if afraid that they are not quite human, or as if the unending queue of distressed relatives and dumbstruck friends has forced her to erect a mask of total indifference. Perhaps she has learnt that it is better not to open herself up to the flood of fearful anticipation or predictable suffering, confessions of things not done soon enough, complaints about doctors' failings or nurses' errors, about the system, about the hospital, about the food.

He eats the chocolate bar before getting back to Sarah, not wanting her to know how he's succumbed to eating comfort food whenever he's away from her.

*Will she smell the chocolate on my breath?*

'Do you remember when we went on holiday to Andros, in Greece?' he asks when he's back in the familiar chair beside her bed. 'I was just thinking about it for some reason. It was such a lovely island. So unspoiled. So perfect. I think it was probably the best holiday of them all.'

Sarah smiles. 'There are better to come,' she says.

'Yes, of course there are! Hundreds…'

And he curses himself inwardly for his insensitivity, for his hopeless, helpless inability to say the right thing, for somehow implying that the best times they would have together are all in the past. 'Hundreds…' he repeats.

He is falling quickly, more quickly every tenth of a second, but Sarah is slowing down.

With her slowness and his speed the distance between them is increasing with each passing instant. How could it be otherwise?

She is slower every time he sees her.

Her fingernails have stopped growing and her hair has fallen out.

In the cycles of chemotherapy the blood cell production of her bone marrow sometimes reduces almost to zero and leaves her susceptible to the slightest infection.

A common cold could kill her.

He's been sitting beside her for two hours and only now registers that something has changed. 'What's wrong,' he asks. 'Why won't you look at me?' So she looks at him. For some inexplicable reason a sudden sense of loss crushes him down into the plastic chair until its metal frame begins to creak. What is it? There is a strange expression in her eyes. Somehow they have lost the magical connection that he's always felt was there, that he's seen there ever since that day on Ealing Broadway, outside the record shop, since the moment he first spoke to her. He struggles with the effort of simply continuing to breathe. 'Nothing can go wrong between us, can it?' he whispers, reaching out and taking her hand.

His voice echoes out across the Avon valley, as pathetic as a child's.

> *Can it?*
>
> *Can it?*

As piteous as the call of a gull.

Sarah is only half paying attention. She is listening to her iPod. She pulls a speaker from one ear. 'What do you mean? Why should it?' She pats his hand. Her fingers feel very cold. *Things are unknitting,* Michael thinks as he continues to fall. *Somehow, for some reason, things are unknitting...*


He is falling quickly but the level of the vincristine in the bag hanging from the wheeled stand at Sarah's bedside is falling too slowly to see. Sometimes Sarah's voice is so weak and slow he can barely hear her. She is dizzy a lot of the time and when she's nauseous it makes him feel nauseous too. Once as she vomited he had to hurry away to the visitors' bathrooms and cough his sparse breakfast into the toilet bowl, overwhelmed by disgust at his own weakness. He can't believe that Sarah can be so calm, so centred, so determined, so resourceful, even now.

He can't believe that he can be so disorganised, so fearful, so confused, so scatter-brained, so weak.

He feels as though there's nothing beneath his feet to support him, to hold him up.

He feels as if he's falling – falling towards the centre of the earth.

## Chapter Seventeen

'I want to be alone sometimes,' Sarah says.

'I'm afraid that's almost impossible in this place. Now, if we'd gone against our principles and taken out private health insurance…'

'I can ignore all these…' She nods towards the residents of the beds around her. 'I can't ignore you.'

'Me? Why would you need to ignore me?'

'You don't see it, do you?'

'I don't see what?'

'You'll have to try to understand, and not be hurt.'

'I can't promise anything.'

'I may be going to die, Michael. You won't admit it, but you know it's true.'

'You're not going to die. I – we – we won't let that happen.'

'You see? You think you can control it. There are some things you can't control.'

'The doctors have this cancer defeated. It was a stage one, and the chemotherapy is just to make doubly sure.'

'Even if the cancer doesn't come back, the chemo may kill me.'

'Of course it won't. How can you think that? Why do you think the nurses hover around you like flies? They're here to make sure that, no matter what, nothing can go wrong.'

'But it may. It may go wrong. You can't control everything.'

'Yes, they can.'

'*You* can't, Michael. *You*.'

'So what am I supposed to say?'

'That you accept it. That I may die. That you acknowledge the possibility and are going to try to get on with your life despite it. That you'll let us both live in the real world – not the world we've always lived in.'

'We do live in the real world. We've always lived in the real world.'

'No, we haven't. You've always tried to protect me. I've allowed it to happen but now I feel – '

'Ill?'

'Michael, please… I feel… I feel as if I want to grow up. I feel as if I don't have much time left, or might not, and in what little time I have I don't want to be protected. I don't want to hide behind you, Michael. I want to look life or even death straight in the face with my eyes wide open.'

'But that's exactly what I've tried to do for you. That's what I've wanted to help you do.'

'There it is, you see. That's what I'm trying to say. I don't want to be *helped*. That's why I need some space, some time when you're not around, day in day out, for every second of my waking existence. I want to take ownership of my own fate, Michael, but you won't let me. This is my illness. It may be all that's left of the rest of my life.'

'Don't ever say that, sweetheart.'

'I want to grow up, Michael. I don't want to die not being a grown up. I'm thirty-four years old and I don't want to die feeling somehow like your child, nurtured by you, protected by you, smo – '

'Smothered by me?'

'No, I didn't mean to say that.'

'Smothered. That's what I'm doing. Smothering you. Rushing over here every day, trying to be here for you, and I'm smothering you… Shit…'

'Shush, Mikey…'

He looks around at the other beds. The other patients – the woman without any legs, the inquisitive crone, the babbling woman – are all intent on their own private suffering. What do they care about him or Sarah? Why should he care about them?

How in fact can you care about anything when the very ground on which you are standing is beginning to fall away?

*What use am I,* he thinks, *if I'm no use to you?*

It's darker down here, only a little way above the surface of the water – and it's difficult to hold fast to your sense of purpose when you're travelling at this sort of speed.

Three and a half seconds is all the time he has. Three and a half seconds from the lip of the bridge to the cold river water…

What was he trying to do? What had he hoped to achieve?

Sarah was his project, his life's work, the only worthwhile project he'd ever had. Sarah was the framework he had used to make sense of things. He had a mother who believed in nonsense and a father who believed in nothing but *he* had found meaning. Sarah had been his meaning, had given shape and form to his life.

*I'm sick of being Michael Germain. Too old to be a whiz kid but far, far too young to feel so jaded...*

*What the fuck went wrong?*

He knew, when he jumped, that the tide was in.

At least he'll hit water, not mud.

But all that stuff about his bones breaking, his spine compacting – most of that won't happen when he hits the water. Most of that will happen when he hits the mud beneath the water.

*Death by mud,* he thinks. *Is that what I've opted for?*

Later that evening he wakes from an uncomfortable slumber in his hospital chair to find a nurse bending over Sarah's arm, taking her blood pressure. Someone does that every three or four hours, even in the middle of the night. They want to make sure Sarah's oncologically poisoned heart isn't going to give up the ghost.

The nurse notices Michael watching her. She smiles reassuringly. 'Amanda' her badge tells him. She's tall, slim, with a lively figure barely veiled by her thin smock. Michael realises he's woken up with an erection. He imagines Nurse Amanda's legs wrapped around his hips. He tries not to stare down the front of her uniform at the exposed curve of her breasts. He imagines Amanda leading him to the bathroom at the end of the ward and methodically unburdening him of his pent up frustration and despair. He imagines her breasts falling free as he unbuttons her smock and his cock springing outward as she unbuttons his jeans.

This is Michael Germain at his poisoned wife's bedside, revelling in images of an undiluted lust.

The nurse saunters away and he turns his head to watch. In his mind he hoists her smock over her hips, runs an imaginary hand up the inside of her thigh. It's only as she turns the corner with a quick glance back towards him that he looks away to find Sarah's eyes on his. With sickening abruptness his fantasy detumesces. He returns

*to the bridge*

Sarah's gaze, attempts a smile, says, his guts churning with guilt, 'Oh, so you're awake.'

He's more than three quarters of the way down and he's feeling unwell.

'How are you feeling?' he whispers.

'There's that question again.'

'I just wish I could do something to help. You know that's all I want to do.'

'Just go home. Make yourself a decent meal. Get some sleep.'

'I don't need sleep anymore.'

'Everyone needs sleep.'

'And when I try to sleep I feel… strange… vertiginous… dizzy. I feel like I'm falling.'

He stands up, walks to the window where he likes to stand, looks out at the window opposite.

*Why can't I be allowed to have a purpose? Can't this be my purpose: Sarah's happiness, her survival, her health?*

In the other building a man walks past the window, a paper file under his arm.

*There are other lives out there,* Michael thinks. *Other lives that work. That are not so embedded in just one other person. That are not so fragile or so utterly dependent.*

Suddenly he wants to get away from this hothouse of emasculating decay, from the inescapable smell of over-cooked food and classroom disinfectant, from the prison of ownership and possession into which he has thrown himself. 'God, I wish I could take you home,' he whispers.

Sarah doesn't hear him.

He thinks she's thinking she won't ever go home again.

## Chapter Eighteen

The wind rushing past him smells of mud and waterweed and cars and stone – but what does he care for that?

Michael is unfettered, un-stuttering, unconstrained, falling to his death.

He is naked to the past, naked to himself – the future means nothing and he's accelerating fast.

This is his act of independence.

Just *this*.

Michael unlocks the front door and backs into the hallway with a dozen bunches of flowers clutched precariously in his arms. He nearly drops the keys, curses, laughs, swings round and heads for the kitchen. Summer is almost over and he barely noticed it passing, but the light falling through the parallel slats of the wooden blinds fills the kitchen with a warm glow. He piles the flowers on the kitchen table and starts pulling open cupboard doors. It's perfectly evident that he's taken leave of his senses. They haven't enough vases for even half of these flowers!

He takes the few he can find, plus a couple of bottles, a couple of water jugs, cuts a centimetre or two off all the stems, divides the flowers amongst his assortment of pots, carries them off to resting places all over the house.

The smell of the flowers – with his nose half buried in a vase of freesias – takes him back to times long before Sarah's tumour, makes of Michael Germain a young man, twenty-four years old, newly-wed.

*God, how good it was to be that man, to be that age, to be with Sarah then!*
*How good life was, how tremendous a gift, how generous a boon!*
*So why is it so different now?*
*So why am I here, falling to my death?*

He remembers as if it were only that morning Sarah clapping her hands with delight as they returned to the house after the wedding reception. 'It's just like Christmas, Michael! Like a hundred Christmases all rolled into one!'

*to the bridge*

He remembers looking from Sarah to the teetering stack of wedding gifts in the centre of the room and back to Sarah again. Her face was like a child's, radiant, amazed, utterly beautiful.

'Come here,' he thinks he said. 'Come over here, my little darling' – like the line from the Leonard Cohen song – and he remembers wrapping Sarah up in his arms… wrapping her up in his arms like the most wonderful wedding gift there ever was.

*This*

*is*

*it.*


*Yes, this:*

    *No failed, half-hearted, faltering, inconclusive attempt at death.*
    *No pitiable, child-like plea for help.*
    *No spineless descent into apathy or depression.*
    *No acceptance of the cards Fate has dealt.*
    *No final capitulation.*
    *Just*
    *this:*


He checks the house over one last time. He's hoovered the carpets, dusted everything, scrubbed the kitchen floor until it gleamed, washed the windows, polished the stainless steel hob…

Everything is as shiny and clean as a show home, all set for the hard sell. He steps out of the front door, pulls it shut behind him, stands there for a moment looking out over Perrett's Park.

There are children in the park, playing on the swings. He can hear their voices drifting up the hill.

How could he be happier?

The last of the chemo sessions is over.

The prognosis is good.

Sarah is coming home.

*to the bridge*

He drives to the hospital carefully, watchful of other drivers, considerate of pedestrians, holding in check a strange sensation of hysteria that is trying to establish a beachhead somewhere at the back of his skull.

*Don't take anything for granted,* it seems to say. *Things may not be as they seem.*

By Bristol Temple Meads train station the traffic slows down to a crawl, then speeds up again on the dual carriageway towards the M32. He turns left before the motorway begins and makes for the Horsefair roundabout and the old council tower block that's now some sort of hotel. He follows the road past the bus station, turns right onto St Michael's Hill. Eventually he finds a parking space halfway up the hill, sticks a ticket on the dashboard, sets off on foot for the main entrance to the Bristol Royal Infirmary.

He feels like skipping, like clapping his hands.

*I mustn't let myself be too optimistic,* he tells himself. *Let's not tempt fate...*

People look at him strangely. He realises he's grinning inanely, like someone on their way to receive a prize.

'I'm off to see the wizard,' he finds himself humming, 'the wonderful wizard of Oz.'

The tide is high and the River Avon is as deep as it will ever be. Cars are moving as slow as snails on the road beside the river. He thinks he can hear a voice – a voice he half recognises – calling out.

Is it too late to phone the Samaritans? he wonders. The plaque on the bridge says, 'Samaritans care. Talk to us anytime, night or day.'

But if he talked, would they listen?

And what's the use of talking now?

~ Son?

    ~ Isambard?

    ~ Good luck, son.

    ~ Thank you, sir. And good luck to you, too.

    ~ I've never needed luck. Work was always what did the trick for me.

    ~ But will work work now?

    ~ At this point in time... it's difficult to say...

*to the bridge*

And it's difficult to speak when you are puffing your cheeks in and out like the bellows of a forge. Smoke pours in great surges from the tip of Isambard's recaptured cigar. His eyes dim and glow, dim and glow, as though there's a furnace raging in his skull...

...as there always was...

...as there still is.

Sarah is sitting in Ward 31, on the edge of her bed, her bags packed, a magazine in her hands.

'I'll just say goodbye,' she says, 'and then we can go.'

'I'll come with you.'

'No. Stay here. Keep an eye on my bags. I won't be long.'

So Michael stays, perched on the end of the bed Sarah has just vacated, feeling strangely desolate. It's peculiar how indebted he feels to this place, how he feels almost afraid to leave it. Afraid to take Sarah away from the safety net of Ward 31.

He waits for Sarah to finish saying goodbye to the nurses and the trainee doctor currently in the ward. He glances at the other patients with their poison-dispensing sacks of liquid hanging at their sides. The legless woman opposite mumbles in her sleep. 'Urba. Urber gurga. Dominer. Gurg.'

The little old lady with the glint of sardonic humour pushes herself upright in her bed by the window to scrutinise Michael more closely. A sleepy contract cleaner lazily aims a brush in their direction.

Michael smiles at the cleaner, picks up Sarah's magazine, lets it fall open in his hands.

### Your partner's pleasure points and how to please him

The attractive young woman gazing out at him from the pages of the magazine has a thoughtful expression on her face, as if racked by one of life's great mysteries.

*Now there's a puzzle...* Michael thinks to himself, turning the page.

*And the puzzle is: who the fuck cares?*

Isambard's bridge, high above them, is as aloof as the smile of a pope. The sides of the gorge and the terraces of Clifton gaze down upon the falling man and his semi-corporeal companion with a frowning disdain. Brunel is behaving oddly. He has his arms outstretched to either side and occasionally glances from one to the other while flapping them, as if trying to judge their wind resistance and the likelihood of their enabling him to fly... but he's more like a scarecrow in a gale than a bird on the edge of taking wing.

~ Don't worry, friend. I have a contingency plan.

~ Then should we feel some degree of hope?

~ Not *we*. No.

When Sarah comes back her eyes are shining with tears. She's hardly cried in eight months of illness and chemotherapy but she's crying now. His own emotion catches like a fishbone at the back of his throat.

'Do you need a glass of water?' Sarah asks.

Half-laughing half-choking he waves her magazine at her. 'No. No, it's okay.' He regains control of himself, throws the magazine onto a chair, picks up her bags, nods a mute goodbye to the woman by the window, then starts walking along the ward towards the exit. 'Let's just go.'

In the corridor outside he suddenly stops. He turns to Sarah, says, 'Can you believe it? You're not a patient anymore. How fantastic is that?'

'Very fantastic, sweetheart. Now let me carry one of those bags.'

'You must be joking. Are you sure you're even up to walking all the way to the car?'

'I could walk to Land's End the way I feel. Give me a bag! I'm not an invalid!'

Michael shakes his head. 'I'm your bag handler,' he says. 'I always have been and I always will be.'

Half a second from impact and Brunel's ghost is having second thoughts. He wavers in and out of vision, shimmers, shivers, seems barely able to control his substantive self. Sometimes he's a puffing, flapping scarecrow, sometimes he's no more than the hint of a top hat, a fizzing cigar, a pair of glinting toe caps.

~ Are you off, then?

*to the bridge*

~ New territory for me, young man, but yes, I think I'm off.

~ Well, thank you for being with me for part of this. It would have been lonely without you.

~ I'm sorry not to be with you at the end.

~ No need to be sorry. You've done as much as was humanly possible…

~ I tried –

But it's too late for conversation. The cigar and the great engineer suddenly go out like a light.

Perhaps he's gone to build pyramids with the Pharaohs, Michael speculates.

Perhaps he's riding the Great Western in the sky.

*~ I tried… the Samaritans… I…*

Outside 59 Sylvia Avenue Michael jumps from the car and hurries round to the passenger side to open Sarah's door. She climbs out with a strange smile on her face, as if there's something sad about coming home as well as something wonderful. She leans against the car door and looks out over the vehicle's roof at Perrett's Park. 'You know,' she says, 'I almost feel as if I've been reborn. As if I'm looking out at the world with new eyes, with the eyes of a stranger, not the eyes of Sarah Germain at all. Everything seems new and different.'

Michael laughs. 'Including me?'

'Yes.' She smiles out at the view of the city. 'You seem the most different of all.'

Michael leans down and suddenly lifts her into his arms. Sarah gasps in surprise, laughs out loud. 'What are you doing, you mad fool?'

'Everything is new,' he says. 'Our life, our marriage, everything.' He kicks the car door shut and carries her up the steps to their front door. 'I'm carrying the new you into our new home for the very first time, just like I did on our wedding day. Just like on our wedding day, this is a wonderful new beginning for us. You'll see…'

Her arms are around his neck and she's looking into his face. He feels an unutterable happiness welling up within him – which is suddenly replaced by a terrible sensation of loss.

He drops the house keys. Almost drops Sarah.

His heart thunders in his chest.

He thinks he's going to faint.

*Sarah?*

Oh, the water is there alright.

Brunel is gone and the water of the River Avon is waiting... is waiting to receive him like the wide open arms of the Lord.

He manages to pick up the keys with Sarah still in his arms. She's laughing, he's quaking in his shoes, confused at the overpowering sensations of happiness and loss, laughing too.

*Oh dear god –*

He's holding her so tightly she's having difficulty catching her breath. 'You're hurting me, Mikey.'

*The all-loving embrace of the Father will receive him like the sea receives the river and the land receives the rain.*

The key won't turn. It won't turn in the lock. He twists it backward and forward, worried it'll snap off in his fingers and ruin their special moment.

Please don't let anything ruin this special moment.

*The Answerer will answer every question until there are no more questions to be asked.*

Then the door swings open and he steps inside, with Sarah in his arms and the smell of flowers all around them.

*And the Taker will take what is there to be taken.*

And Michael is about to hit the water –

– but he hasn't hit it yet.

*to the bridge*

# Part Three
# Impact

*to the bridge*

## Chapter Nineteen

A cold white light will illuminate the river bank later that morning. It will have travelled one hundred and fifty million kilometres from the white hot surface of the sun, passing the orbits of Mercury and Venus, penetrating the ionosphere, the mesosphere, the troposphere, arriving, at light speed, here between the tall bluffs of Clifton and Leigh with the bridge high above and the traffic sweeping past on the far side of the river.

There can be no self-deception, no illusion, beneath a light like this.

The single track railway to Portishead will curve away along the river's edge; roach, bream, chub and pike will nose their way through the disturbed river water… and Michael Germain will drag himself up through mud and reeds to the harder ground on the south bank of the river.

The cold white light will expose every bruise, every cut, every smear of mud or trail of blood on Michael's cold white flesh. It will take pity on his juddering inhalations, on the way he stumbles, shivering, retching, towards the edge of the path. The cold white light – is it matter? energy? a wave that oscillates like sound? – whatever it is that this light is, will it remember the things that earlier light has lit? Will it remember the mothers and daughters on the morning run to school, the commuters on their way to work, the early-bird tourists peering over the bridge's balustrade?

It will remember the first Roman foot soldier to crest the brow of the hill and gaze, with overwhelming wonder, down into the gorge.

It will remember the light that lit the craftsmen as they scaled the careless heights at the bidding of Isambard Kingdom Brunel.

It will remember the very first horse and carriage that clattered across the newly opened bridge.

It will remember the S.S. Great Britain sliding beneath the bridge on its journey to the sea.

But will it remember Michael's fall?

Or will it already have forgotten?

*to the bridge*

Michael fell – and there were arms outstretched to receive him.

God's arms – yes, *His* arms! – were uplifted to receive him.

The river's arms and the arms of the child were raised up to receive him.

Arms of light and the arms of fate were lifted to the humbling sky, outstretched to accept him.

History's arms, knotted with muscle and sinew-tight, were there, held high, to take him.

The arms of heroes and the arms of the weak, fresh from victory and fresh from defeat, were there – who knows why? – to embrace him.

The arms of those who jumped from Isambard's bridge a year ago and a hundred and ten years before were held out to enfold him.

The arms of the Earth and the arms of the Mother were waiting to receive him – were uplifted to receive this gift, to accept Michael's offering, to embrace him and forgive…

The arms of the species – yes, the arms of humanity! – were waiting there to shield him from the impact of the fall, were there to lovingly enfold him, were there to soften the river water, to draw him down beneath the river's surface, were there to draw him, frail but unbroken, down amongst the perch and bream, down towards the riverbed, down amongst the dark green weed, down into the river's mud, immersing him and trapping him and holding him, were there to hold him down until what little breath his fall had left within his lungs had long since ebbed away, until what little thought survived his fall had faltered into stillness, until his interrupted heart had forgotten what it meant to *beat,* until his intercepted body had forgotten what it meant to *walk* or *crawl* or *run* or even what it meant to *swim,* until his undivided soul had forgotten what it meant to long for, to hunger, to dream of, to desire, until all was forgotten and perhaps even forgiven as the flesh of the riverbed parted to receive him and closed once more to hold him tight.

And in that place there was a stillness, a great and wonderful stillness, a peace that he had hungered for, a deliverance that he had sought for almost all his life, but that only now…

…only now…

…in this instant…

…seemed to be his.

*to the bridge*

But then –

Then the river released him.

The river unshackled him from the clinging love of mud and weed. The river unshackled him from the earth's decaying love, from water's suckling hunger, from the ankle grip of clay and shale...

Released him – and turned his mouth and chest towards the air.

Released him – and raised him, perfect as a new born child, up towards the air.

Released him – and held him up, resurrected and renewed, towards a new life.

*I* –

Matter or energy or sound-like wave, light is not cast indivisibly over the surface of the earth.

It is not cast like a shroud over the cities of men.

It does not fall to lie like mist in the cradle of the valley.

Any child knows that.

Light is a bombardment of missiles, shot from the surface of the sun, traversing hostile, empty space at light speed, surviving its perilous journey through Spartan vacuum or clouds of meteorite and dust only to beat down upon the flank of its ancient enemy, its light-bewitched adversary, the Earth.

The water, its surface tension broken, will fall away from Michael like a shroud.

Michael's past – his present, too – will fall away from Michael like a mist.

He will not swim, but somehow he will reach the river bank and, crawling through the seeping mud, reach harder ground. He will stagger up towards the track of the disused railway line.

Will a rescue helicopter swoop to pass beneath the bridge and follow the course of the river towards the estuary, leaving Michael invisible in its wake?

Standing beside the railway line, will Michael straighten his spine and turn, his fists clenched with pain, to look back towards the river – and then look up towards the beetle-browed forehead of Isambard's bridge?

Will no one see him?

*I –*

Gorse bushes and spindly saplings will huddle close to the sides of the gorge. Old flint will brood upon the passing of the river. A single desolate herring gull will forsake its lonely vigil above the Clifton Gorge Hotel and swoop down through the air to vanish behind Leigh Tower.

The earth will wait its turn.

*I –*

The pain of Michael's life, of consciousness, the pain of being human, of being mortal and flawed and weak, the pain of knowing in every success the immanence of death – will this sudden unexpected consciousness ring through Michael's body like the knell of a cathedral bell celebrating the baptism of a child?

*Can I – ?*

The pain in his stomach will be like the pain of an amputation. Anaesthesia will not have been invented. There will be a pain in his head like the pain of a surgeon gone mad.

Michael will reach up and find blood on his lips.

'*Christ...*'

Christ – barely spoken, more croaked than articulated, like the last gasp of a frog half-way down a heron's throat.

Will Michael stagger with the shame of it?

Will he put his hands to his face and weep?

Mildred will say, 'I wonder where he is, what he's doing, that son of yours?'

Jane, almost angry, will reply, 'I know what you're thinking but I don't accept that as even a possibility.'

'Accept what? If you're so clever as to know my thoughts?'

'I could believe it of Roger – of a man like Roger – but not of Michael – not of a man like him.'

*to the bridge*

Mildred, aggrieved: 'What on earth would you believe or not believe of that godforsaken child of yours?'

'That he could run away from the crisis he and Sarah have somehow managed to concoct between them – like his father ran from me. At the first sign of trouble off Roger went, nimble as a bloody March hare. Running was Roger's way of dealing with things, not Michael's. Roger: yes. Michael: no.'

'You've always had such a high opinion of that boy of yours…'

'And you haven't?'

'Me?'

'Haven't you always had a high opinion of him, too?'

'I suppose I have. Yes, I have to confess I have. Of Michael… and of Sarah.'

'So what should we do then, do you think?'

'About what?'

'About staying, leaving, whatever?'

'You are the one who decides important things like that, Jane.'

'Then I think we should pack.'

'Then, dear, let's pack.'


Will the light, expelled like a disease from the surface of the sun, match the light of disease that burns in Michael's eyes?

He will clutch his stomach, staring downwards in confusion at what he's finding there, then stagger to his knees, vomiting bile and water. He will fall, crashing forward to lie on the gravel of the path, his face pressed down into the dust, the smell of stone and vomit invading his nostrils, small creeping things and the cold river breeze exploring his naked skin – and then he will roll over and stare, with wide open eyes, up towards the sun.

No one will have seen him.

He will be invisible.

He will have become the invisible man.

Hours will pass and the rescue services and the fire brigade will scale down their search. The fire fighters will settle on the edge of Downs, eating sandwiches and pouring steaming mugs of tea.

Snatches of their conversation will drift like leaves down into the gorge.

'Don't think this is one for us…'

' – coast guard – '

' – washed out to sea – '

'Or stuck in the mud.'

'Don't be a *stick-in-the-mud…*'

'Ha ha ha…'

'Just some idiot…'

'Bloody fool…'

So this was what he was: unknown male, measured, judged, dismissed.

White complexion, of more than average height, unclothed. Witnessed by a dozen schoolchildren and captured on CCTV. Vanished from the surface of the earth.

When the coastguard report no sightings the divers will arrive. The divers will hunt through the riverbed like salamanders on the trail of a tasty eel snack.

No body will be found.

No one will see Michael lying there, two metres from the riverbank, staring up into the cloudless sky.

No, no one.

He will have become invisible.

After all, no one can survive a fall from such a height. No one can survive a fall like that and not change into something they were not.

'Aa – ' and he will draw his knees up to his chest as the sky grows dark with pain.

Is he some space-station refugee, discarded here by a technology so advanced it seems like magic?

Is he a starman, fallen to earth?

*I know what it was…*

*I know what it was that went wrong…*

What is he, curled here on the river bank? What are the parts of him? What are the signs that make a man? How can we know he still exists? Fingers, fingernails, hair? The uniquely identifying retina at the back of his eyes? Is that the key? Do clothes make the man? Is he naked and so unmanned? Do words make the man? Is what a man *makes* the definition of what he is? Is the thing that crawled half-broken from the mud Michael Germain or is Michael still there beneath the water, awaiting reconstruction in the minds of those who knew or loved him, in Sarah's mind, in

Jane's mind, in Mildred's mind, in the minds even of those who disliked him, who thought him too aloof, too smug or too insincere, too pushy or too certain of himself, or those, contrarily, who found him insufficiently self-promoting? Will this be all that is left behind? A scattering of memories?

Will he curl up like a foetus in the sudden recognition of his loss?

Has he really discarded everything?

*I tried to steal Sarah's illness. I wanted to steal her cancer but I was stealing her identity. I wanted to steal her death. I wanted to die in her place and leave her here, in mine – whilst all the while I was denying her herself. When I carried her into our house, after that final stay in Ward 31, it was not as a bride that I carried her but as a child; not as a lover but as a child in her father's arms.*

Will it begin to hurt more to remain there than to try to move?

Eaten by cold and racked with pain, he will roll onto his side and push himself up, his knees shaking, his muscles barely tame. The putrid smell of mud on his skin and in his hair will stand up with him, closer than a shadow, inescapable as guilt.

Will he really be able to stand?

He will force himself upright.

Will his spine still work? Will his knees still work? Will his bones still fit the sockets where once they sat so snug?

He will force himself upright.

He will stand beneath the burden of what he has become.

*I –*

Will Mildred say, 'God, I so hate packing'?

Will Jane say, 'And I *so* hate unpacking'?

It seems almost certain that Mildred will say: 'Packing's worse.'

And Jane: 'No, unpacking is.'

Will Michael feel his ribs strain against his chest – bird-breasted survivor of an inadequate flight, inhaling the scent of leaves, of car fumes, of old bark – and will he feel nine-tenths dead but utterly alive, somehow rescued, somehow redeemed? Will he remember those times sitting beside Sarah in her hospital bed and feel in the palm of his hand the touch of her fingertips? Will the cold February air burn like acid in his lungs, sear like vincristine, scour like ifosfamide, penetrating the boundaries of the cells of his body and interfering with his DNA – great lungfuls of healing air like an eight month course of chemotherapy?

Will he feel the grating of his broken ribs?

Michael will step forward, his back to the abutment of Leigh Tower, his face towards the city. Can he walk, then, as well as stand? A cough will wrack his chest, beginning with a sound like sandpaper rubbed on stone, ending with the sound of a gurgling sewer. And will he shuffle forward, then stagger, then stumble, then shuffle some more, perfecting his impersonation of a very old man?

How much time has passed?

Gravel will cut his feet as he shuffles – but grunting and gasping and determined not to fall he will stumble on. Where is his zimmer frame? Where is his electric geriatricar?

He will take control of this body of his.

He needs to control this body of his.

There is somewhere he has to be.

Michael will walk along the edge of the river to the dual carriageway, climb up the embankment to the road. He will wait for what seems like an hour for the traffic to clear, the smell of exhaust mixing with his personal smell of mud – and when there are absolutely no cars in sight he will cross the dual carriageway and circle round onto Coronation Road. There is always plenty of traffic on Coronation Road. There is always plenty of traffic everywhere. The cold white February light will steal his invisibility away. Drivers will sound their horns. Seeing him naked, mud stained, bleeding, pathetic, an object for horror and scorn, the drivers will sound their horns. Some will wind down their windows and shout:

'Are you mad?'

*'I'm calling the police!'*

'Get the fuck away from here!'

*'Oi! Fuckhead! What are you trying to prove?'*

'Hey! There are children in this car!'

*to the bridge*

The children, of course, will judge him less harshly. Pre-school and pre-prejudice, they will simply see him as a puzzle, as an unexpected fact that needs to be explained.

*I know what it is I did wrong...*

And will he remember?

He will remember Sarah saying, 'I still love you, Michael. Of course I do. How could I not, after all that we have been through together, all that we've survived.'

He will remember her saying, 'You are my best friend, Michael. Of course you are! There is no one else who comes near to how I feel about you.'

But he hadn't believed her. He had only believed the emptiness of his own soul.

*Oh god...*

As filled with light and death as a messiah newly resurrected from the dead, he will shuffle, stumble, shuffle along Coronation Road towards York Road. A police car will slow down next to him and crawl along the kerb as he walks. A woman constable will stare at him through the glass, suppressing a grin, speaking inaudibly to the driver. Then, rolling down the window, she will begin to ask, 'Are you – ?'

But her radio will crackle into life. The driver will mutter something angrily to the woman, who will nod and the window will smoothly shut. The car will jump forward and race away, its siren beginning to howl.

*What had the police woman been about to ask?*
*Am I – ?*
*Am I what?*
*Am I an apparition, risen from the dead?*
*Am I still human?*

There will be a pain in his stomach, growing worse with each passing moment.

There will be a pain in his head that pulses with the beating of his heart.

But what is pain?

Is there joy and transcendence even in pain?

Had he been right about that at least?

*I –*

*I do not need to be your protector, Sarah.*
*Forgive me for trying to protect you.*

No, that was too self-deceptive. That was far too charitable.

*Forgive me, Sarah.*
*Forgive me for using you as the superstructure for my life...*

Michael will no longer feel his toes or his feet – if he has ever really felt them since the fall – but numbly they will continue to carry him forward over the surface of the earth.

He will no longer feel his ankles or his legs halfway up to his knees. He will lose sensation in his fingertips; pins and needles will course up and down his arms.

But he will feel a pressure that beats upon his shoulders, upon the top of his head, upon his arms – the bombardment of a million tiny missiles dispatched from the surface of the sun. Will he eventually be ground down by this endless photonic assault? Will it wear him down to nothingness, reduce him to an outrageous drunk, a ridiculous, laughable tramp, stumbling, shuffling beside the river?

Will he stagger and fall to lean against the railings, looking down at feet he can no longer sense are there? Will he inhale the stench of the river, of mud and weed and agricultural waste? Will he push himself upright and shuffle on, his body growing weaker but something else inside him growing stronger, like a light that shines ever more brightly, a beacon somehow lit within himself?

Will cars continue by him on their way to Southville or Bedminster, their passengers' faces surprised, eyebrows raised, eyes wide, peering out at this free-fall survivor, this astronaut from another dimension of time and space – and will he feel laughter rising up through the water that still bubbles at the bottom of his lungs?

Will he think, *Why stare at me? Why stare at* me*? Shouldn't it be me who stares at you? Reckless inhabitants of a speeding metal box... Driven compulsives, entangled in the bindings of your seats... Where are you going? Where do you think you are going?*

And *'Ha!'* he will laugh – if you can call a sound that sounds like dying laughter.

*Sarah.*

*I'm coming home.*

Will he remember the bony valley between her breasts, the curve of her ear lobes, the scrap of hair at the nape of her neck, the downy hollow at the base of her spine, her calves, her ankles, each of her fingers, each of her toes… a smile spreading slowly from the corners of her lips…?

Will he remember the way she had cried on the overground to Ealing, stopping, starting, building, rebuilding, like a spider with its web on the wing mirror of a car?

He will come at last to Perrett's Park and looking upward see the terraced roofs of Sylvia Avenue beyond the trees. The houses beneath those roofs covet the families within them. The Avenue, the suburb, the city of Bristol fits its citizens like a glove – inhabitation and love inhaled and intermingled in the same breath.

And will Sarah be there waiting for him at Number 59, wondering where he is, why he has taken all this time to do whatever it was he was doing, why he hasn't made any attempt to phone?

Will Jane and Mildred have arrived, as he thought they might after his phone call to his mother, coming all the way from Cheltenham in order to restore order to the world?

*There is nothing here that a rosary will heal.*

Will they hear a knocking at the door, the impact of knuckles that are numb on the end of arms that no longer feel anything at all?

Will they come to the door, clustering in the hallway, their faces radiant with concern and hope and forgiveness and love, looking out through the doorway into the front garden of Number 59 Sylvia Avenue like the sun revealing itself through broken clouds?

Will the whole street smell of flowers and breakfast and childhood and the whole city waver in and out of existence like a ghost? Will light leap from the windows of the houses on Sylvia Avenue like the light of a lighthouse seen from the decks of a ship lost at sea?

Will he hear his mother's voice and Sarah's voice and Mildred's voice greet him, lapping around him like the waves around a drowning man, like birdsong in the garden of the Lord?

Will he reach out to embrace them and will their arms reach out –

– and will their arms reach out to receive him like the arms of the Wife and the Mother and the Aunt?

He knows what he will say.

He will say:

>*I love you, Sarah.*

>*Jane – mum – I love you.*

>*I love you, Mildred, Auntie M, I love you.*

He knows what he will say.

He will say:

>*I love you, Sarah.*
>*God knows how I love you.*

He will say:

>*I –*

## Chapter Twenty

'Jane?'

'Mildred, dear?'

'Have you tried to ring again?

'Twice.'

'No answer?'

'Just bloody voicemail.'

'What do you think…?'

'What on earth do you mean, *what do I think*?'

'Are you beginning to worry?'

'Not beginning to, no.'

'A lot?'

'I don't know, Millie. How well do I know Michael anymore? I can't believe he would walk away from that woman you seem so fond of. I wished he would for so long…'

'But…?'

'But now I'm not so sure.'

'Has something changed? Have you begun to like Sarah a little more?'

'Perhaps dislike her a little less…'

'Or perhaps even understand her a little?'

'I wouldn't go that far. I'm not sure I understand anyone anymore.'

'My goodness…'

'*My goodness* what?'

'My goodness, is this really self-doubt at last?'

'Would you like it if it were, Millicent?'

'I'm not entirely sure. I don't think I would.'

'You see me as an old battle axe, don't you? Stuck in my ways, inflexible, intolerant. Unable to change. Unable to accept change.'

'Shouldn't I see you that way?'

'No, of course you shouldn't! My intolerance, my inflexibility, my *opinionatedness* are just an illusion that I foster in those who know me. In fact I'm as flexible as a willow, as changeable as the weather, as adaptable as... as someone who is ever so adaptable.'

'Even if I love you for all those other things? For all your Jane-like certainties?'

'Oh, so now you love me?'

'Does that surprise you? Didn't you know? Isn't that why I'm here? Hadn't you guessed?'

'Oh, Millie... I've taken you for granted, haven't I? I'm that sort of person, aren't I...? I've taken you for granted just as I took Roger for granted until he left. And Michael... and even Sarah. Christ, I've taken you all for granted for years and years. That's the sort of person I am, aren't I? A taking-for-granted sort of person.'

'Perhaps,' Mildred will say, and she will lean forward in her chair and pat her friend's thin hand and say, 'But don't cry, dearest. There's no need to cry. It's too late in our lives for tears. You know I've always loved you and you know I always will. Isn't that – don't you think? – isn't loving one another – isn't that enough?'

'Maybe that's a lesson Michael is learning, too.'

'He's about to ring at any moment.'

'Do you think so?'

'I know so.'

And the two women, mother and aunt, will look towards the phone.

*to the bridge*

*to the bridge*

# Acknowledgements

Thanks to the Bristol boys, north and south, for their encouragement and support.

Thanks to David Grubb for his close reading of the text and numerous invaluable recommendations.

Thanks to Juanita Rothman for her many kind words about my writing.

Thanks to Isambard Kingdom Brunel – without whom this novel would not have been possible.

*to the bridge*

# Luke Andreski

## Being Left Behind

Have you ever felt abandoned by the ones you loved? Have you ever felt rejected, excluded or left behind?

*Being Left Behind* is a volume of poetry which explores the relationships between lovers, friends, parents and children, and the feelings of abandonment, love, disappointment and loss which these relationships can bring.

> "A harrowing read." **Michael Bessant**

## Swog

Sigmund Freud meets the Brothers Grimm in a fairy tale for grown-ups, with no fairies, a hero of immense appetite, and a profoundly conflicted giant. Set in a future where civilisation is once again feudal and the Empire of the Outer Hebrides is a power to be reckoned with, Swog sets off on a journey which may lead him to fame, fortune… or death.

> "I love the sheer inventiveness of this novel. I am eagerly awaiting the sequel!" **Sheila Andrzejewski**

## How to be Happy –
## The Maxus Irie Book of Happiness

The Maxus Irie Book of Happiness is a work of fiction. It is a work of humour. It is a serious investigation into ways to be happy.

When you begin reading this book you may find yourself questioning the meaning of happiness. You may begin to question the meaning of cults. You may even begin asking whether either should be considered "funny"?

When you finish reading this book you may find yourself compelled to join Maxus Irie, *the Anticult*.

> "Definite feel good factor from reading this – thoroughly recommend for those seeking more happiness in life!" **Marie-Louise Collard**

Available from Amazon

*to the bridge*

Printed in Great Britain
by Amazon